# TALES OF WAGGING TAILS

## CANINE SHORT STORIES

PEPPER PRESS

First published in 2024 by Pepper Press, an imprint of Fair Play Publishing

PO Box 4101, Balgowlah Heights, NSW 2093, Australia

www.fairplaypublishing.com.au

ISBN: 978-1-925914-99-3

ISBN: 978-1-923236-00-4 (ePub)

© Jim Fraser 2024

The moral rights of the author have been asserted.

Front cover design and typesetting by Ismail Ogunbiyi

Back cover design by Ana Sečivanović

Front cover photograph by Erik Lam

Back cover photographs by Pat Barrett, Nicole Brandes, Kate Grant, Maia Krieger, Bonita Mersiades, Billy Payne, Jane Thompson, Jill Valentine, Helen Yardley

Internal photographs: Aady, Joshua Daniel, Sharon Eade, Jim Fraser, Michael G, T.R. Photography, Kevin Siebel, Jackson Simmer, Amber Turner, Rafaëlla Waasdorp

All inquiries should be made to the Publisher via sales@fairplaypublishing.com.au

A catalogue record for this book is available from the National Library of Australia

# TALES OF WAGGING TAILS

## CANINE SHORT STORIES

PEPPER PRESS

JIM FRASER

To my sisters Christine and Margaret for a lifetime of love and affection, and my partner Sue for her continued support at all times.

# Contents

# A DOG NAMED BEAR

MY FIRST EXPERIENCE WITH WORKING DOGS came when I ran a guard dog company in Sydney. The dogs were kennelled during the day and delivered to building and factory sites at night. Most of the dogs were aggressive—found to be uncontrollable by their owners—and this aggression was utilised in their work. They were quite happy to work behind a fence at night and sleep their days away in the kennels.

Anyone who has owned more than one dog will know that dogs have different characters and temperaments; of course, these guard dogs were no different.

During the time I operated that service, I had incidents on several occasions with many of the dogs, but one in particular was a real character. He was constantly into some type of mischief or another—he was a real rebel.

His name was Bear. He was a German Shepherd who weighed over 45 kg.

Bear was ideal for this type of work. When he came into my care, he was around five years old and a very experienced street raker. He had attacked several people, and his owners had been told by the authorities that he had to be put down, but they settled on using him for guard work instead.

I first realised I had my work cut out with Bear when he was put to work in a paddock over an acre, a holding yard for a local new car dealership. The yard was situated in an industrial area next door to a trucking depot that operated 24/7.

Bear had been at the yard for about a week working with a German Shepherd bitch of similar age, and there had been no problem until a truck from the depot backed into the fence and knocked it over. This happened about 10.00 p.m. on a Friday night when I was out visiting friends with my wife. Bear couldn't believe his luck and made a beeline for the driver caught between his truck's safety and the depot office. Fortunately, Bear always announced his presence, and the driver realised he was under attack before Bear could close in on him. The driver, tired after a fourteen-hour drive from Melbourne, found fresh energy reserves and made it into the office with Bear hot on his heels.

Within minutes, I received a phone call from a rather breathless driver telling me that Bear was loose in the yard and asking me to come and get him. This only posed one problem: I was about 35 km away, and it would take me about forty minutes to get there. I told him to sit tight and left immediately.

As I drove, I worried about what Bear would be up to, and the thought of insurance claims for damage to persons and property was foremost in my mind. Although I hadn't had Bear long, I wasn't apprehensive about him. He had already impressed me as a dog that could look after himself, and to hell with the authorities, his previous owners and me too—in any order he chose.

During the time it took me to drive in, Bear utilised his freedom and the array of human flesh that abounded in the depot to his best advantage. Drivers and loaders on the floor when Bear arrived on the scene were quickly put on to all types of areas out of his reach. Truck cabins, the tops of loaded trucks and all other accessible vantage points were filled rapidly as Bear did the rounds of the depot. Drivers lucky enough to gain a safe spot offered encouragement to their fellow workers, depending on their likes or dislikes for whomever Bear was chasing.

The shouting and cheering that accompanied Bear's antics, of course, spurred him on to greater efforts, and in no time flat, he was Lord of the Depot Floor. Any driver foolish enough to try and establish a more secure position was soon sent back to his original spot as Bear did his rounds. All of this had only taken minutes. With the distance I had to travel,

Bear had everything under control when I arrived.

With the activity reduced to drivers shouting at each other from their safe spots and no one to chase, Bear positioned himself in the middle of the floor and lay down as if going to sleep, but remained alert to any movement—tempting any foolish trucker to run the gauntlet. Safe in their spots, the drivers then proceeded to form a sweep of a dollar per person with the holdings going to the driver who could reach the office.

Two foolhardy drivers reached the floor but were soon put back on their perches by the ever-alert Bear. And then Bear's big moment arrived—or rather, the Head Checker did. The Checker was in charge of the depot at night and ruled his domain with an iron fist and a sarcastic wit that did not endear him to the drivers. He was a man of about fifty, and none of the drivers had ever seen him smile or in a happy mood. He was, in fact, a perpetual whinger who was unhappy with life and so tried to make life unhappy for everyone else.

He came through the door with his ever-present checklist and stood, hands on hips, eyeing the scene. The drivers were not working, and he was obviously not happy with their inactivity. He soon let them know of his feelings.

Bear, experienced campaigner that he was, let the Checker walk past the safety of the office before he acted. Bear's ambush was perfect, as the Checker had nowhere safe that he could reach before Bear. When he spotted Bear, the dog was lying facing him, and the Checker didn't read the situation well. The fact that the drivers were in safe spots and intimidated by the dog didn't register with the insensitive Checker, who just shouted at them to get off their backsides and return to work.

Then Bear reacted. The Checker, with years and years of bossing drivers, stood his ground and waved his clipboard at Bear. Now, Bear wasn't dependent on the Checker for a job, or the best load, and couldn't give a damn for authority of any kind, so the waving of a clipboard was an extra spur to the big dog, who accepted the challenge readily.

Bear circled the Checker and herded him towards a blind corner with a locked roller door, giving the boss no escape. Bear now closed in on the Checker who broke into a run with Bear's growling drowned out by the uproar made by the drivers. At that point, the Checker saw one slim chance of survival. The roller door was operated by a chain hanging by the door and extended up some fifteen feet. The Checker, fleet of foot by this stage, made a frantic dive for the chain and quickly hauled himself out of Bear's reach, with the dog snapping ferociously at his heels as the Checker struggled to establish a more secure position up the chain.

I was still some fifteen minutes from the depot, so the Checker had some frustrating moments as his strength wilted. He occasionally slipped down the chain only to be put back up again with renewed vigour, and Bear almost scored a bite on several occasions.

The drivers' sweep was reorganised, with Bear being quoted at odds of up to 4/1 with the odds rising as the time ticked on.

After a hectic trip through busy Friday night traffic, I pulled into the yard, wondering what problems I would face when I entered the dock. As I walked towards the depot door, I heard the shouts of the drivers as one of them, who had slipped from his safe seat, was put back on his perch by Bear, who quickly returned to the Checker's chain.

Walking into the depot, I was given the impression that I had walked into a sporting event as the atmosphere was typical of a football final or a wrestling match!

Bear and the Checker were undoubtedly the centre of attention, and there was much amusement amongst the men at the expense of the Checker, whose hands were white from gripping the chain for the previous fifteen minutes. I walked up to the dog virtually unnoticed by the drivers, so intense was their concentration on the contest before them.

Ten feet away from Bear, I whistled him to me, and he ran over obediently, wagging his tail and pleased with his efforts. He came to my side and rolled over on his back, legs up in the air in a submissive gesture. This was accompanied by much booing and jeering from the drivers, as they realised the Checker was safe and all bets were off! I snapped on a lead and slip collar and walked Bear to the car as the drivers climbed down from their spots, swapping jokes about the incident.

The Checker regained his composure after he dropped to the ground. He immediately barked orders at the drivers and restored an orderly atmosphere to the depot. As I walked from the door, he said he would like to see me in his office before I left. Placing Bear in the car, I returned to the depot and was stopped by one of the drivers as I neared the office. He told me that the dog was the best thing that had ever happened in the ten years he had been working there—but added that I should be careful of how I handled the Checker, as he was solid with the management and was quite a power.

As I approached his office, I considered my position. Although their driver had knocked over the fence, the trucking company, in fact, owned the land where the cars were stored and may now object to the dogs being situated next door.

I knocked on the door and entered the office. The Checker was on the phone. He motioned me to a chair, and I sat down and pondered what could happen over the incident. The Checker soon hung up the phone and turned to me with a grin—not the reaction I had expected!

"Bloody hell," he said. "That was close. I was wondering how long I could hold on out there! I'm still pretty quick for my age, and it's amazing how much strength a person can find when he's scared!" I agreed with him, a little confused by his attitude. He continued on, almost as if he were talking to himself. "You know, I've been here over twenty years and I haven't got a friend in the place. They all dislike me because I'm the boss and I'm hard on them—and they're right, I am too, but I've got good reason to be. They're a good bunch of men out there, good men, family men, and damn good workers. Most of them are overcommitted with their trucks and have to work long hours to break even. In that situation they are under pressure all the time, and if I gave one of them an inch, they would *all* want to take a mile. No, they don't like me, but that doesn't mean I don't worry about them, and keep an eye open and an ear to the ground for what's going on. That way sometimes I can swing a cream load for someone who is a bit behind with a rig payment but I can't let them *know* that. You see what I mean, son?"

Yes, I could, and I could see that this man was genuine in what he had said. He then continued on.

"That dog probably did us a favour. There has been a bit of tension on the floor and it had to come to a head sooner or later. It happens every now and then. Usually, a fight develops between two of the blokes and after it's over everything returns to normal for a while. This will clear the air for a while anyhow. The only thing I'm dirty on is I couldn't get a quid on myself—4/1 are good odds in anyone's language, and I knew bloody well I wasn't coming down!"

He then seemed to snap himself back to the character I had first seen on the floor and ordered me out of his office as he was busy.

As I walked through the door some of the drivers had gathered around waiting to have their loads checked. Not missing an opportunity, the Checker called after me. "Remember what I said, if I see that bloody mongrel dog here again, I shoot it!"

"He bloody would too, the old bugger," one of the drivers commented. "Old bludger wouldn't think twice about it either," another commented. I didn't answer but walked away, thinking that Bear had them bluffed for half an hour, but the Checker had been doing it for years … little did they know.

Of course, after his victory with the drivers, Bear had to be moved to another yard. This time I worked him in another new car-holding yard, with about a hundred cars waiting for pre-delivery. The yard had been the target for thieves on many occasions prior to the use of the dog service and only the best dogs could be worked there.

Bear and I had struck up a strong friendship by this time as I had recognised him for the character that he was, and he went absolutely crazy when I went to pick him up in the morning. Several times he had knocked me over greeting me and then proceeded to slobber all over me. Any form of obedience for a compound dog of this type is out of the question, as obviously we did not want somebody breaking in and telling the dog to sit and stay while they committed theft, so it was always difficult to contain Bear's greeting to a point where I didn't suffer in some way or another. Bear had to be trained to stay back from the fence so he could not be looped with a noose and then tied to the fence, so it was about a week later that I moved him to the new yard.

As I pulled up in the afternoon the yard foreman was preparing to leave and he was most impressed by Bear's size and disposition behind the fence. I let Bear and the bitch he was working with into the yard and stood and watched as he patrolled his new area, cocking his leg over everything and anything that was slightly of interest. Driving off I wondered whether he would behave this time.

The next morning, I arrived back at the yard and Bear was nowhere to be seen. The bitch was waiting at the gate and I whistled to Bear, wondering whether he may have dug out from the yard. Then I noticed him down the bottom end lying on the roof of one of the new cars! He noticed me about the same time and jumped up, happy to see me. I had visions of the top of the car being scratched by him as he jumped down, but worse was to come.

Bear always took the shortest route to me when he saw me, and this was over the top of the cars. Showing remarkable balance and speed for his size, Bear proceeded to jump from roof top to roof top, and each time he hit the roof with the full weight of his 100 pounds plus.

The car roofs suffered varying degrees of damage and I stood helpless to stop him. It almost seemed a lifetime as I watched him approach, anxious to be with me. As he hit the last roof he slipped and rolled heavily off the bonnet of the car, denting that for good measure, and jumped to his feet, as if he had not suffered at all from the fall, and pinned me up against the fence, leaving a trail of scratches and dents in his wake.

I led the dogs to the truck and went to survey the damage. It was mostly scratches and minor dents with only two cars suffering major dents to their roofs.

Sitting over a cup of tea later I told my wife about the incident, saying we would probably get a call from the yard with a cancellation of the service because of the damage. Sure enough, the phone rang later and Ted, the yard foreman, was at the other end.

"We had a bit of trouble here last night; somebody got over the fence. That new dog's good, mate, he kept them up on the roofs of the cars and chased them back over the fence. They won't be back, that's for sure."

"Much damage?" I asked.

"Yes, a few roofs and a bonnet, but better than losing another car. Our insurance premium goes up every time. Anyway, I thought I'd let you know that the big dog's okay." Seems like Bear had nine lives.

Bear's next move was to a large semi-government yard where I thought he may stay out of trouble … but of course that was wishful thinking. The yard contained a workshop area which was enclosed, with very little in the yard, and I thought, *nothing he can damage by climbing on.* All fences were intact, and I had never had a dog escape from the yard since we started the service. But of course, the fence was not Bear-proof.

On entering the yard, I walked Bear around the perimeter of the fence, checking as I went to see that there were no holes, and letting Bear explore his latest home. The fence-line bordered onto another semi-government installation which was staffed at all times by watchmen. There were four watchmen who worked a rotating shift, and all were older men; two were, in fact, retired policemen, and three of them were obese to the point of being breathless if they had to move around a lot while carrying out their duties.

As Bear and I approached the corner line where the yards met, one of the watchmen was on his rounds.

I nodded my head to him as he approached, and he acknowledged me with a wave and then, spotting Bear, called me to the fence. Without any form of introduction he said, "I could kill him, you know. I am an ex-Commando and they showed us how to do it in the last war; easy when you know how."

Now, I had heard this line many times before and I wondered just how many Commandos were trained in the last war. It seemed if ever we worked a patrol dog in a public area there was always at least *one* Commando present who was quick to identify himself and tell me how easy it was to put a dog out of action.

Of course, the war had been over some thirty years by this stage, and time had not been too kind to our ex-Commando who, even if he had retained his training, would have lost some reflexes as he put on the pounds, and he wasn't talking about an ordinary dog, he was talking about Bear—speedy, aggressive and downright sneaky along with it.

Not waiting for me to comment he continued: "Better not let him near me, I'll fix him."

He then shook his fist at Bear who of course reacted to the agitation in a predictable manner. "Yeah," he said. "You can bark while you're on that side, be a different story if you were in here."

He then kicked the fence, and Bear really reacted. The watchman then walked away, muttering about the useless bloody dog as Bear's aggression subsided and he turned to sniff alongside the fence where the man had kicked. He lifted his leg and marked his new territory, at the same time looking over his shoulder at the disappearing watchman.

As I grew more familiar with Bear's habits I often marvelled at the dog's incredible body language and the way he showed utter disrespect for people in some situations, as we had just encountered. I hadn't said a word during the one-sided conversation, and I wandered off to complete my inspection of the site.

Bear worked at that yard for a period of a month without incident, and I started to feel secure about his location, but of course he was only lulling me into a false sense of security. The one thing I learned about Bear was that he was an opportunist, and if given the chance, he would quickly take advantage of a situation and act upon it—always to his own benefit.

Sunday was always a full day for me as the dogs were loose in most of the jobs all day. I used the time to mend fences and kennels and do any other maintenance that was required. It took me a full day to get around to all the jobs.

One Sunday, after Bear had been on the new job for a month or so, I arrived on site and Bear was nowhere to be seen. His workmate, the bitch, was on the job and greeted me happily at the gate but a search of the yard showed that Bear had left for parts unknown. I walked around the perimeter of the yard looking for a hole in the fence, or some indication of how he had escaped. Then I found a hole dug under the fence, near where I had encountered the watchman, and this led into the yard where the watchmen had their little office.

Cursing Bear I started searching for a way that I could gain entrance. The sun was beating down unmercifully with temperatures around the 38° mark, and again I cursed the big dog, wondering what I was going to encounter.

Sweat pouring off me, I climbed over the fence and worked my way towards the one-man office, hoping that the watchman was safe inside. Turning the corner, I spotted Bear immediately. He was sitting outside the office door, relaxing in the sun.

As I approached, I noticed that Bear was situated outside the only door in the hut. I had visions of the watchman inside, sweltering in the heat, and I wondered how long he had been bailed up. I called Bear as I neared the hut, and he stood up, lifted his leg, looked over his shoulder at me and then ran over—wagging his tail, quite happy with his effort.

I snapped a lead on him and walked over to the door of the office, only to find not one, but three of the watchmen sweating it out in the hut, which closely resembled a sauna bath. Bear's timing was always excellent, but this time he had excelled himself. He had managed to catch the three on a change of shift—two men on the change, and one supervising. They had spent over two hours inside the box and were not *at all* pleased with their stay.

Not wishing to test their patience any further, I decided to retreat as quickly as possible. I almost managed to do so without them noticing me, except Bear wished to announce his departure and his renewed barking brought my presence to the attention of the well-steamed watchmen. As Bear was in the lead and under some sort of control, their imprisonment was over and their safety seemed assured, their anger was obvious.

Spilling out of the hut almost in unison, they vented their fury on me with all types of threats being made to my wellbeing. Bear revelled in the confrontation, and any physical threat to me was out of the question as a safe distance was kept by my fat foes of the moment.

Fortunately, their spell in the hot hut had left them all exhausted and they quickly ran the course of their heated comments. At this stage I interjected, and suggested that the ex-Commando had created the situation by his continued agitation of the dog, adding that he was responsible for the situation—not me. The dog, I explained, had never caused this type of problem before (dog trainers are apt to stretch the truth at times) and he was provoked into the ambush.

I took this opportunity to leave as the other two guards, seeing the logic in my statement, had turned their attention to our Commando who was defending himself valiantly as I ushered Bear through the hole under the fence.

As I repaired the fence I mused over the history of Bear, and in all of his missions outside of the fence, I realised he had never actually *bitten* anyone. He had intimidated a few, of course, and his presence when he was aggressive was very fearsome, to say the least, but he had not one bite to his name.

Bear was on the move again. Not wishing to stretch my luck with the watchmen, he was moved to an isolated industrial area. For the first few weeks all seemed fine, then I turned up one morning to find Bear had gone walkabout.

I started patrolling the streets, criss-crossing the area: no trace of Bear. The only sign of activity at the early hour was outside the local private bus depot where the drivers were queued up waiting to gain entrance.

I passed the drivers twice before I realised that the buses usually left before I picked up the dogs. That familiar feeling of dread hit my stomach and I knew, without a doubt, that Bear had something to do with the buses running late.

Because of previous incidents, I was a little shy of situations where I became the object of anger due to Bear's escapades. I drove the van around the corner and came up with a plan that would let me escape the wrath of the crowd. Leaving the van parked, I took hold of a lunch box and walked towards the depot.

As I neared the depot, I saw Bear standing behind the wire gates, defending his newfound territory. The drivers were standing around engaged in conversation, each suggesting some solution to the problem, while the depot manager was almost beside himself.

My plan was to ingratiate myself with the men by solving the problem and removing Bear without them realising he was *my* dog. To do this I had to speak to the foreman before Bear noticed my presence, as I knew he would act all coy and give the game away if he noticed me. I approached the foreman as Bear renewed his barking at a driver who had ventured too close to the fence line.

I walked past the now nearly demented depot manager as if I were on my way to work. I then turned to him and asked if he had a problem with the dog. All the time I was silently praying that Bear would not notice me and give the game away, but I had no worries as he was engaged in his favourite pastime—harassing anyone within twenty feet of him.

I asked the depot manager why someone didn't just go in with the dog and get him out so that they could all start work.

"Are you joking?" he replied. "That bloody mongrel would tear your arm off."

"I don't think so, those dogs are usually just bluff. Most of them back down if you stand your ground with them," I said, keeping my voice as quiet as I could so as not to attract the barking dog's attention.

A glimmer of hope sprang into the eye of the depot manager. "I don't suppose you could do it, could you?" he asked in a pleading voice.

I hesitated for effect and then said, "Well, I don't know, I'm running a bit late for work myself."

Following up on his only hope he continued: "Mate, I've got twenty-three buses running late and hundreds of people waiting at stops all over the place. My job will be on the line over this."

"Well, I'll give it a go, I suppose, but I can't guarantee anything," I said quietly as I moved through the drivers towards the fence.

Bear was flying full force towards the fence, venting his fury at a driver who was trying to coax him around. I burst through the drivers and screamed at the dog who dropped to the ground as if he had been shot.

Bear was lying submissive on the ground as the gates were opened, and playing my part to the end, I edged through the gate and grabbed a firm hold on the dog.

The men rushed through the gate, hurrying towards the buses, and the manager hesitated as he walked past. "You handled that well, mate, almost as if he knew you."

"Just the way you talk to them—I'm a country boy. They used to say I had a way with animals at home," I replied in my most innocent voice. "What do I do with him now though, I'm already late for work?" I said.

The manager's mind was already on other things. "Let him go down the road somewhere," he said as he hurried off.

I breathed a huge sigh of relief as I walked Bear back to the van, and headed for home.

Some breeds of dogs go through an extended juvenile stage and mature very late. Labradors, Afghans, Dobermanns, are often said to be neurotic because of this late maturity. Most of these breeds mature around about two and a half years of age, and of course, cause their owners much frustration in the meantime.

Bear never was one to stick to the rule book. German Shepherds usually mature early and an eighteen-month-old dog is considered an adult. The fact is, Bear never quite made it out of the juvenile stage, which of course caused me a few frustrations over the years.

When Bear reached the age of eight, he was afflicted with a severe kidney complaint and this necessitated him going on a course of medication to stabilise the condition. At this stage I decided to put Bear into semi-retirement. He would no longer spend his nights behind a fence in a factory or car yard, but relax in his kennel, at home, with his former partner in crime—Gypsy.

Semi-retirement for Bear was also not without incident. His biggest shortcoming as a compound dog was that he was an escape artist of consummate artistry, and it was in this area that I decided to utilise his talents. Any new job was tested to see if it was Bear-proof.

After checking the fences and any other areas that were likely areas of escape for the dogs, I would let Bear loose in the job and wait outside in the truck. If Bear didn't turn up within an hour, I could be confident that the job was escape-proof. If there *was* a way out, Bear would quickly find it, and be back at the truck, showing that familiar body language of tail hooked over his back, leg cocked on anything that was near, looking over his shoulder at me with his head tilted to one side. After that it was a matter of placing Bear back in the job, and following him to see where he had escaped from.

Bear settled into kennel life easier than I thought he would, and he spent much of his day sunning himself in the exercise compound, and the nights in his kennel yard. The only real problem I had with him at this time was if I left him behind when I took the other working dogs out at night. Twice, when I retired him, I left him at home and all hell broke loose. Bear barked non-stop while I was out and succeeded in stirring all the other dogs in the kennels into a chorus of barking and howling which could be heard from a considerable distance.

After two such disturbances I learnt the error of my ways and Bear accompanied me whenever I took the dogs out to work.

Bear, being Bear, moved from the kennels, onto the back of the truck, to the front seat of the truck, and spent most of his journeys with his head on my lap, only raising his head when something outside the truck created an interest.

Bear had been on the kidney treatment for almost two years without any noticeable change in his condition; he was eating well and keeping his weight. I had got into the habit of letting him and Gypsy out in the morning when I first got up, and letting them run loose while I walked up the drive and picked up the newspapers. We were living on a five-acre block and the drive was about 100 yards from the house, so the run was broken up with frantic chasing and play-acting between the two dogs as they released their pent-up energies.

Gypsy would always come immediately when called, whereas Bear would stop, lift his leg, look over his shoulder and come in his own sweet time. During these morning walks to collect the papers, Bear surprised me by showing his potential for retrieving. He quickly learnt to run up to the gate and collect the papers, and bring them back to me—well, almost back to me, and I sometimes got them straight away, depending on what sort of mood the big fella was in.

As Bear had never had any obedience training, I decided to harness some of his energy to my advantage and teach him to retrieve the papers, just so I would not have to walk up the drive on cold winter mornings. Now, I have never been a believer in food reward for training but in this case, it was a matter of horses for courses, and considering Bear—a master criminal in his own right—I decided that bribery by way of food reward was the *only* way to go.

The system worked well. I would let Bear and Gypsy out of their kennel, return to the house and pour some warm milk into dishes outside the back door. The dogs would then play outside the door until I walked down to start the kennels about half an hour later. I should have realised that any change of the system would bring about a problem, and so it happened in a very simple way. One morning after letting the dogs out, I went to get their milk only to find there was none left. I walked out of the house empty-handed, and Bear looked up at me and licked his lips in anticipation.

I knew I had some canned milk down in the feed room, so I walked past the dogs and headed for there, intending to get some to give the dogs their treat. As I walked down, the dogs followed me, with Bear obviously unhappy with the situation. I disappeared into the shed and came out a couple of minutes later with the can of milk, only to find Bear missing. I had a sixth sense of foreboding regarding Bear's activities, but I shrugged it off, as there was nothing he could do to cause me a problem here (or so I thought). Walking back up to the veranda I was relieved to see Bear heading my way with the paper clutched firmly in his mouth, then as I walked up the stairs, I spotted my two papers where I had left them. Bear associated his reward of the milk with the fetching and returning of the papers, and when no milk was forthcoming, he went to the property next door and stole their papers!

He dropped the paper at my feet and drank his milk, after going through his routine of leg-lifting and looking over his shoulder at me, of course.

I didn't realise it at the time but that was to be the final chapter in the life of Bear. That night, after taking Bear with me on the dog run, I placed him and Gypsy in their kennel and went off to do the rounds of the kennels, checking to see that the other dogs were all bedded down. As I passed his kennel again, he barked at me and cocked his leg on the gate. I opened the door and went and sat with the two dogs for ten minutes. They competed for my attention as my mind wandered back over the incidents that the big, loveable dog had been involved in. I gave the dogs a final pat and walked up to the house. Over dinner that night I said to my wife that I wouldn't know *what* to do when I lose my two dogs. She asked what made me say that. I replied that I didn't really know, it was just that I had received so much enjoyment (coupled with large proportions of anxiety) from Bear and Gypsy, and that I had such a lovely, close relationship with them.

The next morning, I walked down to the kennel as usual to let the dogs out, and as I turned the corner, only Gypsy waited at the gate for me. I knew instantly that the big fella had passed on, and when I opened the gate, my worst fears were realised. Bear lay stretched out on his blanket—his ailing kidneys had finally collapsed.

That afternoon I buried Bear outside my office, where I sit and relax and have my cup of tea on a sunny day.

Often as I sit there now, beside my old mate, I recount his deeds to unbelieving and astonished people, and as I do, I can still see him in my mind's eye. I often smile as I think of the doggie St. Peter as Bear walked up to the doggie Pearly Gates, lifted his leg, looked over his shoulder surveying the situation and looked for a way out.

# ODE TO THE BEAR

The Bear stood tall, the Bear stood proud and when he barked, he barked real loud. He'd cock his leg and urinate on any fence, on any gate.

The meanest dog I ever saw he weighed a hundred pound or more,
This canine didn't give a damn for regulations made by man.
He bit someone one sunny day, the police said put that dog away.
So, he became a factory guard, lord and master of industrial yards.
This dog lived life without a care, but trouble seemed to follow Bear.
He found gaps in a fence one night and scared some truckies into flight.
Around the depot he chased his quarry, some into rooms, some up on lorries.
He then lay guard upon the floor, till the boss man walked in through the door.
Bear licked his lips in anticipation, this was a lovely situation.
A fat old man was easy meat for a dog like Bear who moved so fleet.
Give the boss some due, he stood his ground, then realised that tactic wasn't sound, The Bear had ambushed him just right and no escape was left in sight.

The Bear closed in to have a bite and put the boss man into flight.
The luckless man ran round the floor but couldn't find an open door.
The truckies revelled in the boss's bad luck, The betting ranged from five to fifty-five bucks.

Would the boss man find safe ground or be a victim of the hound?
The boss he lapped the floor again and then he saw a swinging chain.
His only hope to gain some height or suffer the indignity of a bite.

Like a monkey up the chain he climbed, with the Bear a foot or two behind.

He reached safety at ten feet or so, but the Bear was lurking down below.

The betting now began in earnest as the boss's strength was put to a test.

His knuckles clutching at the chain, he slipped then climbed back up again.

His strength was ebbing, his fate seemed sealed, but he gained a timely repeal.

The handler came and saved the day and locked the angry dog away.

All bets were off, the race was run but still the truckies had some fun.

They'd seen their boss humiliated, some wished he had been mutilated.

This canine really was a rebel, The reincarnate of the devil.

Humans, dogs or pussycats, none were safe from this dog's wrath.

So, the years rolled along and at last he grew old, but he did not quieten down but grew more bold.

The list of his deeds could fill a page or three, but his luck always held, and the Bear remained free.

Then he passed along, but where did he go? To the kennel in the sky, or the one down below?

I don't think it matters as I'd bet my life, wherever he is, he's causing some strife.

# THE TWO ROSES

MY WORK AS A DOG TRAINER GIVES ME THE OPPORTUNITY TO MEET MANY PEOPLE, and because my work entails private lessons, I often make lasting friends of my clients. Many of my clients are elderly, and their dogs are often the objects around which their lives revolve. Because of the love these people have for their canine companions, many are concerned that their pets will outlive them and be left with an uncertain future.

I couldn't estimate the number of times over the years that a worried owner has contacted me to discuss this very matter. Usually, the request is made for me to look after the dog, as the owner is sure that the dog wouldn't be happy with *anyone* but me. Unfortunately, this would not be practical, as these dogs are nearly always spoilt lapdogs who roam the house at will, and demand continuing attention. Even if I could accommodate *all* the dogs in my house, I would need to devote my entire time to the dogs for them to be happy. The good news is, these dogs are usually easily placed with another older person in need of companionship—the dogs normally transfer their affections, and feel secure in their new surroundings.

I received a phone call one day from an elderly client for whom I had trained a young Cocker Spaniel some years previously. The lady asked me to come to her place as she had a problem with which she hoped I could help.

Before leaving, I looked over the dog's history card to refresh my memory and left wondering what the problem was. The lady, a spinster in her late sixties, doted on the dog who returned her affection threefold. This was a model dog–owner relationship.

The lady was waiting for me at her front gate, and I was taken aback at the physical change in her since I had last seen her. The lady was a shadow of her former self, and I gathered my composure while sorting out my book and pen in the car before I alighted and approached, trying to hide my feelings.

When I was training her dog, the lady had been smart-looking, alert and active with a matronly figure, topped by a smiling, open face with a double chin that bounced and rolled as she giggled behind a closed fist. Now she had undergone a dramatic loss of weight, and her once strong figure was covered with sagging flesh; her bones poked out through red blotches, which affects many in our elderly population.

Her gaunt face showed an ever-present pain and her eyes were sunken and lacked the dancing gleam which, along with her giggle, had been lost forever.

She ushered me through into the lounge room and sat me down as she prepared a pot of tea in the kitchen. I watched her labour through the task, sensing that she would be upset at any offer of assistance. The tea made, she sat down and faced me while a grim smile passed fleetingly over her lips.

She came right to the point. "I don't have to tell you that I am dying—it is quite obvious, isn't it?" She then continued, as I sat quietly, thankful of her composure and obvious acceptance of the situation: "I have a malignant growth, and the doctor has given me a month at the outside." She hesitated and took a sip from a glass of water on the table before she continued again: "The problem is the dog. I have no one who can look after her, and do what must be done. I have no immediate family, and most of my friends are old, and it would be unfair to ask them anyway. I was hoping that you might be able to help us?"

While she had been talking, I had already made some mental notes about the dog's age and temperament, and the possibility of placing her. I felt the urge to reassure the lady, regardless of the fact that the dog was now over ten and may not transfer its affections too easily. But I knew, as sick as she was, the lady was still in control of her faculties, and I would not be able to fool her with an off-hand reassurance.

I thought carefully before I answered, searching for the right words. "I think I can help," I said. "It won't be easy to place the dog in a situation where she would be as contented as she is here, but I can certainly try."

The lady blinked in acknowledgement, hiding her mouth behind her hand as I went on. "Firstly, I need some up-to-date information on the dog's habits and its medical history, and then I will make some enquiries."

I completed noting down the information over a cup of tea, and some small talk, and, as usual, when placed in this type of situation, I cursed myself for the inability to make conversation flow in my normal manner. I was packing my things together when the lady arose from the table and stood clutching the back of the chair. "I am terribly sorry to trouble you, but I have no one else to turn to, and I am afraid I can't even offer you much money to look after her."

I shook my head and picked up my papers. "Money is the least of the problem. If the worst came to the worst and I couldn't place her in a home, she can stay at my boarding kennels. She wouldn't have all the comforts of home, but she would be in the company of other dogs, and

get plenty of affection from the kennel girls. When would you like me to pick her up?" I asked.

"I would like to leave it as long as I can. The doctor tells me I will have to go into hospital sometime shortly, and I would like to keep her here until then, if that doesn't inconvenience you?"

"Of course not, it's okay. You just ring me when you're ready."

I reached for the door handle and felt a tug on my arm. I turned. The lady had lost her composure and was on the point of breaking down, but she quickly pulled herself together with obvious difficulty and said, "No, I've changed my mind—I am being a selfish old lady—I would prefer if you took the dog now, if it is possible …"

I really wasn't prepared for the change of mind, but the situation and the lady's incredible fight to maintain her emotions was making me emotional. I readily agreed.

"She is in the backyard," she said. "You can go out the side gate when you get her—her lead and collar are behind the back door."

Having said that, she turned and left the room, closing the door behind her and leaving me standing in the hallway.

I found the lead and collar behind the door and let myself out into the yard. The old dog was lying under a tree in the shade, its legs quivering in its sleep and its breathing shallow and laboured.

I reached down and patted her, and she woke up, firstly smelling my hand, and then licking it in recognition. She slowly rose to her feet and nestled her head into my lap as I knelt beside her, stroking her as she continued her licking and nuzzling.

I ran a practised eye over her body, and noticed she was underweight. Puzzled by this, I ran my hands over her and then found what I had feared—the dog had large lumps under her mammaries and my mind recalled that the dog, according to the details I had just taken, had never been desexed. Her condition now was typical of many older bitches who are not desexed early, and I suspected that she had mammary cancer.

I quickly picked her up and left the yard by means of the side gate and placed the dog in the passenger seat of my car. As I opened the driver door to get in, I glanced at the house and noticed that the lady was looking out through a curtain which had been pulled back slightly. By this time, my emotions were getting the better of me, and I did not acknowledge her presence as I felt that she did not need a cheery wave at this moment.

Goldie crawled over and placed her head on my lap, making herself comfortable, seemingly oblivious to my state.

I needed confirmation of the dog's problem, so I headed for a vet friend of mine who confirmed my suspicions. We discussed the problem at length and, as the dog was not in any obvious pain, we decided to try and make her as comfortable as possible, until she was in pain.

Goldie never did go into the kennels: she made herself right at home in our house and her good nature and quiet ways made her a true pleasure to have around.

I rang her owner after I had Goldie home a day or so, and she seemed pleased, but a little bit off-hand when I told her she was at our home, and settling in just fine.

Over the next two weeks Goldie showed no signs of pain and, in fact, took to following me around the property and waiting patiently for me while I finished my training and other jobs—never demanding, but happy just to be near me and receive either a verbal acknowledgement or a pat on the head and a rub of her tummy.

Then I received a phone call from her owner who had been admitted to hospital, and on the spur of the moment, I made arrangements to visit her at the end of the week. After hanging up, I again marvelled at the strength of character shown by this remarkable woman who, even though she knew her time was limited, still showed concern for her canine companion of many years.

Within a day of this call, Goldie showed signs of stress while walking and lying down, and I watched her closely as she followed me around as I did my morning kennel inspection. Before I had completed my rounds, I realised that Goldie's time had come, and I loaded her into my car for her final trip.

Driving to the vet with Goldie's head on my lap was no easy task as I recalled how many times I had said to clients, "When your dog's in pain, it is unfair to hang on for your own benefit. The dog must come first if you really love it, and if it is in pain, and there is no medical solution, the dog should be put out of its pain." These words always sounded so convincing before, and yet now they seemed so *hollow*.

At the vets, I lifted Goldie out of the car, and she lay in my arms, nuzzling her head under my jumper as we walked through the gate. On impulse, I stopped halfway up the path and put her down on the grass for her last walk around. Back arched in pain, she sniffed around the garden before returning to me and lying at my feet, tummy up in a natural submissive position, waiting for her rub.

Although I only had her company for a short time, I had grown attached to her—perhaps more so because of the circumstances with her owner. She was in every way the perfect companion—a stately old lady of the canine world. On entering the surgery, my vet friend realised the situation, and quickly ushered me into the surgery, closing the door behind me.

Goldie, trusting to her last breath, nuzzled my hand almost as if in a farewell gesture.

The trip home with Goldie seemed to take forever, and as I buried her a little later, I realised that I would not be able to hide her death from her owner when I visited her at the hospital. I gave this matter much thought over the next few days without reaching any solution, as there was no easy way to tell her owner the truth.

By the time I reached the hospital on Friday, I had worked myself into a real state, but had decided to tell the lady the truth, as she would certainly read through any fabrication. I hesitated outside the ward and almost didn't go in, but I braced myself and walked in, aware of the smell that only hospitals seem to have—that antiseptic clean smell that always seems so sterile yet full of foreboding.

The lady was propped up in bed dozing lightly as I approached. Grateful for some respite, I sat quietly beside her for some minutes before she awoke and was aware of my presence. "I am sorry," she said. "Have you been here long?"

"No, not long," I replied, forcing myself to meet her eyes. I sat there searching for words, words that I had been unable to find before, and now seemed impossible.

"Did she suffer much?" the lady asked.

I looked up, shocked that she had been so perceptive. "No, only for a few hours right at the end. I had her put down when the pain came."

"I'm so glad. She deserved that much. She was such a good little dog. I am so sorry that I caused you such a problem, but you see, I couldn't face it myself. I am not a very strong person."

My thoughts raced back to our initial conversation at her home when she said, "The problem is the dog. I have no one who can look after her and do what must be done." She had *known* all the time, and although she could come to terms with her own imminent death, she could not cope with her dog's predicament.

I left the hospital marvelling at the lady who managed to put her pet before herself, and her capability of retaining her dignity throughout.

The lady passed on soon after without me seeing her again. Within a day I received a letter, hand-delivered by one of her friends.

It contained a handwritten note in an almost illegible scrawl from her obviously weakened hand. The note was brief, apologising for any upset that had been caused, and thanking me for my help in a situation that she couldn't handle. The note also contained a twenty-dollar note towards my expenses incurred, with an apology for not being able to give more.

I spent the twenty dollars on a rose bush which marks Goldie's grave. I have never been really interested in gardening and have never planted anything that survived, except that one rose bush, which flourishes 'til this day—a tribute to two remarkable ladies.

# MRS WHITE

I PULLED UP OUTSIDE THE ADDRESS GIVEN FOR MY FIRST JOB of the day—a consultation on a male cattle dog pup who, the owner claimed, was a little overactive.

The house was an old weatherboard, built around the turn of the century; I was greeted at the gate by a small, middle-aged lady wearing a scarf knotted like a turban, with a cigarette dangling from her mouth. "You the dog trainer, love?" she called without changing her expression. I told her I was, and she nodded her head a couple of times before continuing. "Well, I hope you know what you're doing because Big John's had enough of the dog, and if you can't do something with him, he's gotta go."

She turned away and headed for the house, and as I followed dawn the path, I couldn't help but compare her appearance to television show characters in soap operas who lean on the fence talking and gossiping to their next-door neighbours or anyone else who would stop and listen.

On entering the house, I noticed that without being in any way dirty, it was easily one of the most disorganised houses I had been in—stacks of newspapers seemed to grow from every chair or ledge available, and articles of all sorts, types and sizes were scattered about in gay abandon.

Mrs White led me into the kitchen where she sat down, indicating a chair for me. "We'll have a cuppa before you meet the dog, love, something to steel your nerves." She shrugged and went on. "Big John wants the dog to go but I heard about you on the wireless, so I thought we'd give you a try, but Big John says we're wasting our time and money."

As she talked, I watched, fascinated by her constant reference to her husband, Big John. Mrs White was the type of lady who evokes an immediate feeling of warmth in people, and I really liked her open and relaxed manner. She could have been everyone's grandmother; however, her attitude changed every time she mentioned her husband and I had visions of Big John as being a seven-foot-tall giant spitting blood and guts—the type who ate dog trainers who didn't get results for his breakfast.

I suggested to Mrs White, prior to my arrival, that she leave the dog outside until we had completed our consultation, so that I could get all the details regarding the dog without interruption. From outside, while we were talking, the dog was scratching at the door and barking and whining—continuously demanding attention. Mrs White sat hunched over her cup of tea without referring to the noise from outside, and answered my questions with constant referrals to the dog's confrontations with Big John.

During the discussion I ascertained that the dog had been treated by the local vet for hyperactivity with a treatment of diet, hormone injections, castration and tranquillisers in an emergency. Mrs White said she wasn't sure whether the tranquillisers were for her or the dog, but stated that none of the treatment—separately or collectively—had made any difference to the dog's behaviour.

At this point, the moment had arrived for me to meet the dog and I was more than a little interested to study his reaction and behaviour. Normally, an owner tends to exaggerate the problems with an active dog and a program of obedience, owner education, firm handling and a demonstration of leadership qualities by the owner will (in most cases) modify the behaviour to a satisfactory level, so I sat confident in my ability to face the task ahead.

Mrs White left her chair, gave me a resigned look and then opened the door. For a moment nothing happened, then the dog bolted through the door faster than a greyhound could leave a starting box. The dog continued his run, circled the kitchen without paying any attention to me, and headed down the hallway into the lounge room with me following him, awed by his speed and agility as he traversed piles of newspapers and any other obstacle littering his path.

I can only liken the dog's behaviour to that of an animal in a cartoon who runs up walls and across ceilings—with no thought to gravitational forces, nor risk to bodily harm. Mrs White stood leaning on the doorframe, puffing away at the cigarette which seemed to never leave her mouth. She shook her head and looked at me with an amused smile. "Thought I was exaggerating a little, didn't you, love?" I nodded my head without answering, amazed by the acrobatics of the dog who had now turned his attention to me. I managed to grab hold of his collar and slip a choker chain over his head and gain some semblance of control.

Mrs White was suitably impressed by even *this* small amount of control, and I headed for the front door, telling her I wanted to take the dog down to the park to see if he was receptive to my training methods. I invited her to come along; however, she declined with a shake of her head and a smile that suggested I was on my own.

A popular saying of mine is "Don't jump in the deep end of the pool unless you are a strong swimmer", and as I struggled to gain control of my new pupil, I wondered about my swimming ability in this particular case.

At the park, the dog showed remarkable ability with the basic training exercises. I have often found that this type of dog responds *exceptionally* well when shown strong leadership qualities. When owners are given instructions on handling, and educated to understand their dogs (thus eliminating the frustrations that go with owning this type of dog), in most cases a satisfactory result can be attained.

On returning to the house, pleased with my progress, I sat with Mrs White with the dog lying at my feet (with my foot firmly placed on the lead) and enjoyed another cup of tea. I explained that the result at the moment was only an illusion, and that the dog was not yet trained—and a lot of work and patience on *her* part was required to achieve our goal.

Over the next week we had several lessons, with the dog progressing at each lesson, and Mrs White showing a determination and dedication which allowed her some control over the dog, both at the park and while walking on the street. During these lessons constant references were made to Big John and his doubts about our success, and as yet I had not met the gentleman in question—and to be honest, I had no *desire* to face Big John and demonstrate the dog training.

On the day of the fourth lesson, I arrived at the front door of the house to be told by Mrs White that Big John had taken the day off work and was in the kitchen. On being given this information my stomach did a flip, and I followed the shuffling Mrs White down the hall, wondering what to expect.

My expectations of a seven-foot giant were immediately shattered as Big John was a man of normal size and stature and of very friendly nature. (I later enquired of Mrs White as to the reason for Big John being called 'Big John'. Her reply was given with an expression which suggested that I should have understood the obvious. Her *son's* name was also John; thus, they became Big John and Little John.)

Big John watched the dog working begrudgingly and offered no praise or support for our joint efforts. The dog, Mrs White and myself all worked exceptionally well, but Big John was suitably unimpressed by our display. His comment later at the kitchen table over the inevitable cup of tea was, "He's foxing, mate, he's a smart little bugger. I'm not knocking you as a trainer, but no one can train that little bugger."

Big John then dismissed the dog from our conversation, and we spent an enjoyable hour discussing football, with Big John showing a deep knowledge of the game and an easy solution to the problems of his team. Every time I tried to steer the conversation back to the dog, Big John skilfully avoided the issue, until it was time for me to leave for my next appointment. At the door Big John shook my hand and said I should call in any Saturday and we could watch the footy together. He then disappeared, leaving me with Mrs White, discussing our next appointment.

As I travelled to my next job, I thought about what had eventuated, and couldn't believe that Big John was not impressed by the improvement seen in the dog. His intense dislike of the dog was so apparent that I decided to question Mrs White at our next appointment and find out why the animosity in this man was so great.

Before starting our next lesson, I sat with Mrs White who told me of the relationship between Big John and the dog. She stirred her tea idly and thought deeply before starting her story. "Well, love, I suppose it happened right from the time we brought the little fella home and he sicked on Big John in the car. He never did like that sort of thing, you know. He even used to leave the room when Little John was a baby and I had to change his nappy. Then the pup used to annoy Big John all the time, you know, nipping at his heels, stealing his socks. He even ate Big John's good slippers. Big John wasn't happy about that, you

know, not happy at all."

At this stage I thought back to when the dog entered the house at our last lesson and made a beeline for Big John. The dog was obviously delighted to see his master, but Big John didn't share the same feelings, and he lashed out at the boisterous puppy with a well-aimed but somewhat slow kick. The dog easily dodged his foot then ran between the legs of his helpless attacker and nipped him on the other foot. Big John let out a roar which intimidated me somewhat, but was ignored by the dog who was revelling in the game with his master.

"See what I mean?" spluttered Big John. "The little bugger's mad!" The dog offered no respite and continued to attack the feet of Big John, whose efforts to kick the dog had lessened somewhat as he struggled for breath. The thought of all this had brought a smile to my face and Mrs White brought me back to the present by saying, "You can laugh but it's a serious business—Big John treasured those slippers." She then continued: "You see, Big John's only got three things in life that he calls luxuries, apart from his slippers, and the dog's destroyed all three things for him."

I asked what they were in my most serious consulting tone. "Well, Big John's a gatekeeper down at the mill, and he's on his feet all day so that when he gets home he likes to lie down and have an hour's sleep before he goes up to the pub. He's got crook kidneys, you know, so they give him hell by the end of the day, and he really looks forward to that sleep. Been doing that since we were married forty years ago. But the dog won't let him sleep—he scratches at the bedroom door and barks and cries until Big John comes out. Between Big John shouting and swearing and the dog barking, it's a real ruckus, I can tell you." I had visions of the dog, an outrageous attention-seeker, enjoying every *minute* of these skirmishes, plus the tired frustration felt by the hapless Big John.

I asked had she tried to keep the dog out, to which she answered, "Of course we tried that. The first time I locked him out he jumped through the kitchen window, knocked me washing up all over the floor, and Big John wasn't half mad, I can tell you. Of course, the next day I locked the window but he gets under the house now and barks under the bedroom so Big John can't sleep. Causes a lot of trouble, that dog."

I could really sympathise with Big John, with bad kidneys and no afternoon sleep, and I thought twice about asking what else, after ruining the slippers and sleeps, the dog had done; however, I thought, *In for a penny in for a pound*. "What else has he done, Mrs White?"

"Well, Big John likes a bet, and he used to sit on the toilet and study the race form. At first the dog just sat outside the door and barked and annoyed him. Once Big John gets in there, nothing used to shift him, so he ignored the dog and persevered with his race form until one day, the dog got down the end of the hall, ran towards the door and flung himself at the door. The ageing catch gave way and Big John, crouched forward reading his form, was hit on the forehead with the full force of the door." The stunned punter was more than fair game for the happy little dog, who smothered him with affection before Big John recovered sufficiently to eject the dog and regain some composure.

Mrs White relayed these stories to me with a deadpan expression while I, with the thought of Big John being ambushed in the toilet by his dog, was struggling to keep some type of sympathetic expression on my face. Mrs White continued: "Didn't affect Big John and his betting though. He still gets his winners up regular, except now he studies his form at work; safer, you know." I then thought that nothing else could outdo these stories, and maybe Mrs White was pulling my leg; however, she must have read my mind as she was quick to point out that this was all true.

Then came the final, third episode of this tragic story of Big John and his tormentor, and again Mrs White continued: "You know Big John loves his bath—of a night, lies in there for an hour at a time. Says it really relaxes him." My mind raced forward at this point, anticipating what Mrs White was going to say, and I asked with disbelief, "You aren't going to tell me that the dog ended up in the bath with Big John?"

"Yes," she said. "What a mess—and the *language*: I can tell you, I was so embarrassed to go out on the street the next day—everybody in the street must have heard the language!" *Poor Big John*, I thought—*no sleep, no bath and petrified in his own toilet. No wonder he doesn't like the dog.*

The next two lessons went very well and with our course finished, and Mrs White and the dog both doing well, I left her with instructions to ring if she had a problem. I felt quite confident with Mrs White, as her ability to handle the dog was excellent, but I couldn't help but wonder if Big John would forgive the dog for its past trespasses.

About two months later I was in the area and decided to call in and see how things were going. I hadn't heard from Mrs White in this time and presumed that things had worked out okay. At the door I was met by Big John himself who welcomed me in as a long-lost friend. "G'day, mate, come on in and have a beer. The missus is up the shops." I sat down and could not see or hear any sign of a canine and asked how things were with the dog.

John never batted an eyelid as he replied, "He is gone, mate, had to send him up the country to a farm. Little bugger, he was good for me but drove the missus mad. She couldn't do a thing with him. Have you got time to stay and watch the footy?"

# BIG JOHN'S LAMENT

Big John he was a simple man,
He had but modest ways.
A sleep after work a nice hot bath
and a five bob bet each way.
His peace was shattered one fine morn
when a puppy came to stay.
A lively pup with amazing speed
who liked to jump and play.
Now John was gentle, John was kind
but his patience it wore thin.
as the puppy made its presence felt
by wrecking everything.
First his afternoon nap was lost
as the dog made such a din,
that John was forced to get up
and he aimed a kick at him.
The dog, he saw that as a game
and ran around and round,
then jumped right up upon big John
and knocked him to the ground.
Now Big John studied the racing form,
the toilet was his retreat.
The dog howled loud outside the door
but Big John retained his seat.

The dog would not be beaten,
The dog would have his way.
He launched himself at the toilet door
from fifteen feet away.
The door was old and brittle.
The hinges weak with age.
It shattered and it hit Big John
and he bellowed loud with rage.
Amid the ruins he sat there,
a lump upon his head.
The little dog it wagged its tail
and then it turned and fled.
John's dignity was lost now
and he slumped there in dismay.
The dog returned and wagged his tail,
he wanted but to play.
For days thereafter John would try
to catch the wayward pup,
but the pup was way too quick for him,
Big John was out of luck.
The final straw it came one day
as in the bath John lay.
The dog he found the door unlatched
and entered right away.
Big John he lay in silent bliss,
completely unaware,
that the puppy lay in ambush,

it really wasn't fair.
The trap was sprung, the dog it leapt,
Big John's defence was quite inept.
The dog it landed with such force,
then wagged its tail, showed no remorse.
The din was heard from far and near,
John's language was blue and wonderfully clear.
He cursed at the dog so loud and so long,
the crowd gathered outside and wondered what's wrong.
John thought his home should be his castle
and not be shared with a canine rascal.
So a home was found for the pup far away,
Now big John has a bet and a sleep every day.
John pondered on this situation,
The dog had caused him consternation.
His patience it had reached the end,
and all because of man's best friend.

# RICHARD

ONE OF THE PRIMARY PREREQUISITES FOR A GOOD DOG TRAINER IS PATIENCE. If a trainer is impatient with a dog and the dog is sensitive—as many dogs are—the trainer will not gain the trust of the dog, and the training program will then be *much* more difficult for both trainer and dog,

It is the trainer's job to teach the owner how to handle the dog as part of the training program, and this often requires more patience than the actual training of the dog!

Over the years, I have experienced many problems with owners while teaching them to handle their canines. Some people become inhibited the minute they are shown something that is new to them. Others cannot remember their left hand from their right! While others have a shorter concentration span than their dogs.

One job really challenged my patience. Before the program, I had talked at length on the phone to the mother of the man who owned the dog.

The man was in his late twenties and had an intellectual disability, but he was able to converse and was also under treatment for hyperactivity. To keep their son occupied, his parents had enrolled him in many types of activities run by various council and voluntary organisations.

The young man enthusiastically started every course, but it wasn't long before his disruptive behaviour frustrated the organisers, and he was reluctantly asked to leave.

In desperation, the parents tried home tutoring, but the young man showed a wry sense of humour, and his tutors became the butt of all types of pranks until they, too, lost heart and failed to return.

The delighted prankster took each new tutor as a bigger challenge and treated their departure as a major victory. His dog, a five-month-old Boxer, was purchased as a last resort by the harassed parents, who were despairing of finding a hobby to occupy their son's time.

The local obedience club had been most sympathetic to the parents' problems and had endured the enfant terrible for three weeks before suggesting to the parents that their son was not compatible with any instructor in the club.

The dog, at five months, seemed to be growing bigger by the hour, and was very active, and of course his master's hyperactivity stimulated the dog to bigger and better things.

The Boxer had been purchased to help ease the situation with the son; however, the son had instead found a very able ally, and the parents now had double the trouble.

When training on a commercial basis as I do, the easy way to extend your training knowledge is to take on the difficult jobs, and the combination of boisterous dog and incorrigible owner appeared to be a challenge I couldn't refuse.

On the morning of the first lesson, I parked my bike outside the house and found my client waiting for me at the gate. My first impression was that he was as eager to assess me as I was to assess him! His mother rushed from the house to introduce us and send us to our neutral corners, so to speak, then ushered us into the house.

As we entered the door, Richard turned and ran his eyes over my bike, hesitated as if deciding upon something, and then turned to me with a disarming grin. "Nice bike, I like motorbikes." He then turned on his heel and hurried inside, not waiting for my answer.

Richard's mother had tea and scones prepared and I studied Richard as we talked over the various aspects of training and the problems the dog was having with walking on the lead.

Richard was fascinating. The extent of his disability was difficult to gauge as he conversed very well and asked some very intelligent questions. He was very well dressed, and I noticed that he constantly brushed at his clothing or adjusted a button or collar.

As we talked his eyes never left me, staring at me, not even attempting to hide his contemptuous attitude.

During the time it took to fill in my information sheet on the dog, he chose either to answer my questions with stony silence or go into elaborate and lengthy detail about some other aspect of the dog's behaviour. This meant that the information I required at the start of a contract took a long time to gather, and then when we were finished, Richard produced a book and insisted that he would take down all the questions and answers so he could remember them for later.

As he stated, he was looking for some reaction from me, but I had expected an early challenge, so I patiently went through the questions again and purposely missed the section on feeding, for which I was loudly berated.

The observant Richard! I was mildly surprised by his aggression. I had made my first mistake by underestimating my trainee, but I had learned what I wanted—Richard had a very good memory.

Meanwhile, Richard laboriously wrote everything down in elegant block letters, during which time I drank a whole pot of tea and overindulged in his mother's delicious scones.

Richard then asked to be excused for a moment and disappeared out the back door, returning within a couple of minutes. I thought he had gone to the toilet, but I soon learned differently.

The discussion over, I placed the dog on the lead and we headed down the side passage towards the park opposite the house. Richard was in front and watching me as I turned the corner and had a full view of the front lawn. My motorcycle, which I had polished with loving care on the previous afternoon, was being soaked by a very heavy spray from the garden sprinkler. I then realised where Richard had gone previously, but I was determined not to let him gain a point. I showed no reaction, and we walked past the motorcycle, talking cheerfully about the dog's behaviour.

During our lesson at the park, I noted that Richard had difficulty coordinating his hands and it was only if I stopped him and told him what to do, along with a demonstration, that he could grasp even the most basic handling exercise.

Although I remained patient and reviewed each exercise many times, Richard soon became impatient. His frustration grew by the minute, and I suggested that we give the dog a rest. I sat and talked to Richard for a few minutes, and he seemed to relax, so we resumed work.

This time, I suggested that Richard walk to the park by himself and work the dog there. This was much better, as it turned out. Richard, like a lot of other people that I have instructed, was just very self-conscious.

The lesson went well from that point on until we started teaching the dog to stay. I demonstrated the 'down stay' first, dropping the lead beside the dog and returning to where Richard was standing. Richard assured me that he knew what he was going to do and walked over to the dog in a confident manner. He did a fair job of the exercise and then returned to me, beaming with what I thought was satisfaction at a job well done. *Silly me!* After explaining some minor handling errors, I returned to the dog to demonstrate the correct way to handle him.

As I approached the dog and went to pick up the lead, I noticed that Richard had carefully placed the lead in some fresh droppings from another dog. Without altering my pace, I circled the dog and returned to Richard. "I think you should try that again; you almost had it right," I said. Richard looked me straight in the eye. "I can't remember what to do, and you told me to ask if I didn't know."

I picked up the long lead I used for recall work and returned to the dog, unclipping the short lead and leaving it on the ground as I worked the dog on the long lead.

After completing the exercise, I decided to call it a day, and Richard and I headed for his place—leaving the short lead where it lay.

I completed the lesson and wrote down some training exercises for Richard to practise. Then, I gathered my gear and headed for the bike, with Richard tagging behind, obviously looking for a reaction to the sprinkler.

I approached the bike without comment, placed my gear in the saddle bags, took out a cloth and wiped down the seat and tank. Richard stood silently, watching closely for a reaction, and when none was forthcoming, he turned on his heel and left without any farewell.

I waved cheerfully as I left, smiling at the departing figure but inwardly breathing a sigh of relief. Richard was one demanding customer.

Lesson number two hit a sour note very early: we had completed the theory, and Richard took out his notebook and prepared to take notes, as he had done in the previous lesson. I had anticipated this and had prepared some typed information—I produced these pages with a smile and found that Richard had quite a temper. The tantrum that followed was impressive, to say the least, and Richard's disability had not excluded him from learning some quite bad language, and he proceeded to berate me in the very best that he could call to mind.

Richard's tantrum had all the style and rage of a three-year-old, and while his mother tried in vain to quieten him down, I sat unmoved by his antics.

When his rage had abated, I picked up the lead and headed for the backyard to collect the dog. I looked over my shoulder, and Richard sat in the corner sulking. "Come on, Richard," I said in a demanding tone. "We will walk the dog to the shopping centre to see how he reacts around traffic."

Richard looked up at me, eyes blazing in defiance, and then changed his mood instantly, smiled slowly as he fell in behind me and said in a cheerful voice, "I like walks, I like the shopping centre, there are lots of people down there." What he said sounded innocent enough, but a cold chill ran down my back just the same, and I wondered what I had let myself in for.

We walked down to the shopping centre without incident, and while I tried to converse with him, Richard kept quiet the whole time, giving no indication of whether he was listening to me or not.

As we approached the busy centre, I explained the training exercise we would complete and what result I expected from the dog.

The local schools had just finished for the day, and the bus stops in the shopping centre were flooded with children and their school bags. the noise from the children was only drowned out by the rumble of the buses and huge semi-trailers that ran through the centre.

The dog pulled a little on the lead but overall reacted very well, considering the commotion around him; Richard remained singularly unimpressed by his dog's reactions.

The return trip through the centre was progressing well, and the dog had adjusted to the noise and was padding beside me. Most children had left via the continuous stream of buses that wended their way through the heavy afternoon traffic.

I decided this was the perfect time to rekindle Richard's flagging interest and suggested that he might like to walk the dog through the centre and home. Richard took the lead and smiled, showing enthusiasm for the first time that day. I smiled smugly, congratulating myself on my timing.

Richard was talking happily and handling the dog well, but as we approached a crowded bus stop, we had to walk through the maze of people. I noticed that Richard shortened his grip on the dog, severely restricting it and causing it to react and swing around out of control.

I quietly suggested that he loosen the lead to regain control, and he threw another tantrum. Although the first tantrum had been impressive, it was not in the same class as this one.

Richard had a captive and sympathetic audience, and he was experienced at this sort of opportunity—and like all good actors, he was going to milk his audience for every drop of sympathy he could evoke.

"You're always picking on me!" he cried in a plaintive voice, ensuring that the audience got the idea that I was definitely the bad guy. He continued: "I never do anything right as far as you're concerned; are you going to hit me now or wait till we get home like you usually do?" He certainly got the desired reaction from the crowd, as they looked at me angrily, shaking their heads in disbelief that I could be so unfair to a person with an obvious problem.

It takes a strong person to hold their ground and ignore the reaction I was getting, and at the time, I lacked the courage, shrinking like a violet under the stares of the crowd. Richard continued his wailing, winding the crowd up to its limit; he then turned on his heel, dropped the lead, and ran through the crowd, leaving me in a state of stunned silence—and the object of scorn from an irate mob.

Richard and the dog disappeared through the crowd at a rate of knots, and Richard showed a sidestep that would have made some football players envious. He darted through openings between the shoppers, with the dog following in joyful pursuit.

Trying hard to maintain composure, I walked after the wayward duo, cursing myself and Richard as I quickly made my way through the angry mob.

As the crowd thinned, I realised that I could not still see Richard or the dog. I looked on either side of the road, but neither was in sight. Depression set on me quickly as I ran through the complications of my predicament.

At the shopping centre's end was a small grass area with a toilet block and several seats. As I approached, I was relieved to see Richard sitting there, smiling at me, his tantrum over. The dog, however, was nowhere in sight; Richard was lying back, relaxing, almost basking in the sunlight with a mischievous grin that I had come to know meant disaster for me.

He let me know immediately where I stood. "The dog's gone, you're in *big* trouble, my mum paid a lot of money for him—and you lost him! You're in big trouble with my mum—your fault, your fault!"

*Why me,* I thought plaintively, *why me, what had I done to deserve this?* I wallowed in my misery with the same intensity as Richard was revelling in his delight.

My mind began to function again, and I looked around for a sighting of the dog, but he was nowhere to be seen amongst the milling crowd in the shopping centre or in the surrounding areas.

The toilet was a possible spot, and I walked into the Gents hoping to find the dog there. A quick search of the urinal area and the stalls only gained a blast from an irate man who thought my search a bit thorough.

As I walked back outside, Richard was obviously perversely enjoying the situation. I realised that any appeal to his conscience was out of the question. I stood beside Richard and began to remonstrate with him in my most reasonable voice, struggling to control my building anger.

The gent from the toilet then appeared, summed up the situation and added his thoughts to complicate my growing dilemma further. "Is this person bothering you, son?" he asked

Richard, who could see all sorts of possibilities in this intervention. "He lost my dog," said Richard softly. "He lost my dog, and I'll get into trouble."

The gent was not impressed—first, he felt I had invaded his privacy by searching the toilet, and now I had lost this poor boy's dog. He was not a big man and not too young, but he was a seasoned campaigner with a quick and cutting tongue, and I knew I was about to get both barrels from this stranger who had come to young Richard's rescue.

My despair was deepening by the second, and I could think of no way to gain control of the situation. Not only was the dog gone, but Richard was also entrusted to my care, and I could not walk off in search of the dog and leave Richard alone.

Richard had quickly established a rapport with the old man, and they both eyed me with open hostility, comrades in arms, with me as the common enemy.

This confrontation with the old gent had only taken seconds, and then my attention was diverted by girlish squeals emanating from the ladies' toilets. Two young girls ran out laughing. *The dog*, I thought, *The dog is in the Ladies' toilet.*

I headed for the toilet door with the old gent on my heels. "No, you don't, I won't stand for that, you keep out of there or it will be the police for you!" *He's right*, I thought; it would never stand up in court. I had a quick vision of me standing in the dock explaining: "Your Honour, I thought my dog was inside; he likes cool places on hot days, you see, sir." I could see bold headlines in the night's papers: 'Dog Trainer Pervert Trapped in Ladies' Toilet'; the public affairs and investigative television programs would have a field day. My business would be ruined.

Snapping back to reality, I called out to the girls, and they confirmed that the dog was inside, tied in a cubicle. They agreed to release the dog and soon returned with it in tow. I was relieved—but the situation was not over yet, as the old gent was not about to give ground.

"What's wrong with you then? If I were a few years younger, I'd soon cuff your ears," he said admonishingly. "You look like a rogue and a ruffian, and there will be more trouble for you before you're too much older." With that, he turned and walked off, muttering about perverts in public toilets.

Richard had retained his seat and was much amused about the whole situation. My discomfort at the hands of the old fellow had been the coup de grâce in Richard's eyes and the icing on the cake for his little effort.

The walk home was completed in stony silence, but Richard's mood seemed to be entirely happy. He cheerily waved to some friends on the way. He never mentioned the incident to his mum, and I left in a daze, again cursing myself for taking on this job against my initial better judgement.

To my surprise, the following three lessons took place without incident, and Richard developed a style of handling that, although a little unusual, showed that he had become a competent handler.

Encouraged by this unexpected turn of events, I worked hard on the handling, and Richard extended the exercises so that he could handle the dog in almost any situation. We never attempted off-lead work out of the house or in an enclosed area, but Richard and the dog had developed into quite a team, and I was more than a little proud of the result.

On the day of the last lesson, Richard's mum and dad and a proud aunty accompanied us to the park. Richard put the dog through its paces with the aplomb of an experienced show handler. Returning to the house, we sat in a group and had tea and cake. Richard's mum expressed her appreciation for the result, commenting that she thought I might have had more trouble with her troublesome son.

I gathered my gear, said my goodbyes, and walked down the path for the final time. I was filled with a feeling of accomplishment—*a job well done in most difficult circumstances*, I thought. Then I heard Richard call out to me. He walked down the path with a half-smile and stopped before me. I waited for what I thought would be a peace offering, a word of thanks from my disobedient pupil.

Then Richard's expression changed, and he became serious. I waited patiently as he thought of what he would say, and I appreciated how difficult it would be for him to express his gratitude. "You have not won, you know, I wanted to do it for me and the dog; you have not won." With that, he gave me that damn half-smile and turned and walked back towards the house.

I placed my gear in the saddlebag and mounted the bike, angry with myself for being so smug and then being cut down to size. The bike's motor roared to life, and I slipped into gear and turned around to head for home. As I passed Richard's house, he was standing on the front lawn, arms folded and that damned smile plastered on his face.

I rode away into the dusk, feeling like a horse ridden hard and put away wet!

# AN ODD JOB

I$_T$ was my favourite part of the day. I was settled in front of the television—a plate of bacon and eggs in front of me and a steaming hot cup of tea by my side. I had trained six dogs over the day, and each one had been a difficult session, my last session being 30 miles from home, and on the way home I ran into a storm. Riding a motorcycle on a nice day is a sensation all of its own, but at 9.00 p.m. on a cold, wet winter's night, it leaves a little to be desired (even for an ageing

motorcycle enthusiast).

My last client had arrived home late, so by the time I *finally* arrived home I had missed putting my children to bed—that, coupled with a head cold and a running nose, meant I was not in the best of moods.

Now, after a hot bath, and relaxed for the first time that day, I settled down to watch a movie that I had been waiting to see. The opening titles of the movie came on just as I was mopping the last of the egg yolk off my plate with a piece of bread. I glanced at the time, 10:30 p.m. *At least I won't get any more phone calls now,* I thought, but before I had time to pick up my cup of tea the phone *did* ring and destroyed my contented feeling. My wife walked past to answer it; I called out to her if it was a client to please take a number and I would ring back in the morning.

The movie started with John Wayne looming onto the set, resplendent in cavalry uniform, astride a huge chestnut horse, and I settled further into my seat, savouring the feeling of relaxation that was now upon me. My wife entered the room with a look of concern on her face. "There is a lady on the phone with a problem—I think you should talk to her."

I shouldn't have been surprised. It had been *that* sort of a day, and I knew that the problem must have been serious, otherwise my wife would have dealt with the call and not bothered me. I rose from the chair as John Wayne was being chased by two or three hundred screaming Indians and I wondered at the disrespect shown by an unknown client interrupting the movie at such a delicate moment. By leaving the lounge room door open and extending the phone cord to its maximum and balancing precariously on the breakfast bar, I found I could follow the progress of the 'Duke' while talking to my late-night caller.

The lady on the phone was obviously distressed. She owned a two-year-old Terrier who, for no apparent reason, had attacked either her, or her husband.

The attacks had been indiscriminate initially, with both the lady and her husband victimised by the dog at varying times. Now the dog had turned its aggression exclusively to the husband, who was threatening to have the dog put down unless a solution could be found by the weekend.

We discussed the problem at length during which time I managed to keep track of John Wayne's fortunes as he cut a swathe through the Indians *and* fought a saloon bar brawl in quick succession. The lady certainly had a problem but unfortunately, I did not have any free appointments for the next three weeks.

I explained to the lady that I could not fit her in for three weeks and she pleaded that the dog would be put down by the weekend unless I could fit her in. Then she played her ace card.

As I flicked through my diary to see if I could rearrange some appointments to fit her in, I heard her crying, not into the phone in an obvious way, but muffled behind a hanky or something—loud enough for the sound to carry down the phone line. Me, I'm a *sucker* for tears. Like most husbands, I have the occasional set-to with my wife and stand my ground at all costs until the hint of tears appears, and then I buckle right under. The fact is, I can't stand a woman to cry, and now the woman who had inspired such uncomplimentary thoughts from me only a few minutes ago when she disturbed my movie had played a winning card at the right moment.

So, as John Wayne was almost dead from thirst in the desert, 100 miles from help, I arranged an appointment for the following night at 9.00 p.m. I settled down in my seat again just as a commercial came on and my wife asked me the outcome of the call. I told her, and asked had she noticed the beautiful speaking voice of the lady? We speak to many people on the phone from all walks of life and areas of our city, but this lady had such an unusual voice you almost felt that you were talking with royalty. Her phrasing of sentences was flowery and yet did not seem out of place with her, for some reason. She had told me that her residence was set well back from the avenue, but that she would leave the drive lights on so that I would have no trouble negotiating the lengthy driveway, which was lined either side with poplars. The name of the house was on a nameplate beside the entrance, she had said, and that I should have no trouble finding her place.

As I rode over the next night, I wished that I had been able to make the appointment earlier as this was my seventh job for the day. I had left home at 7.00 a.m., and now some thirteen hours and 200 kilometres later, I was feeling the effects of a long day.

As I often do when going to a new client, I imagined what the people were like. I often found that the image generated by speaking to someone on the phone seldom matches what they were like. However, I felt this one was easy. The lady's voice and manner indicated a teacher of some type, or maybe a professional person with a private school background, and the house, from her description, was a mansion, set well back on an oversized block with a sweeping drive lined with the poplars she had mentioned.

As I turned the bike into the avenue and changed down through the gears, slowing so I could catch sight of a street number, I noticed that the area was not one of large blocks and expensive houses but was lined with neat, smaller-type fibro houses with the occasional brick veneer—certainly not the area that had been described by the lady on the phone.

At this time, I reached the number I was looking for and stared in disbelief. The mansion that I had imagined was an untidy fibro house with the garden overrun with weeds, and the lawns running wild. The driveway had three or four trees, naked of leaves, lining the side, hardly the big blooming poplars that I had imagined.

I alighted from my bike, checked my diary and confirmed the street number; then remembering the sign the lady said was at the entrance, I searched for it in the darkness. It was there all right, and, seemingly in keeping with the appearance of the place, it hung at an angle—tarnished and neglected.

I collected my consultation sheets and a pen, and headed for the door, somewhat amused by my overactive imagination, but as I was soon to find out, the night had just begun. That was just the first of many surprises in store for me.

My knock on the door was answered almost immediately, and I tried hard not to look shocked at the lady who answered it. Standing before me was a person best described as having an intricate hairstyle held together by large pieces of junk jewellery which gave the lady a larger-than-life appearance. Her face was heavily made up with a thick white powder, bright red lipstick and heavy rouge. Her eyes were not lacking attention either with false black eyelashes hiding a thick blue tint, and the eyebrows layered on with a black pencil with a somewhat heavy hand.

Recovering from my initial shock, I introduced myself and was ushered into a large lounge room furnished with antique furniture. The lady then started to relate some of the problems with the dog and as I sat, fascinated at her appearance, it seemed to me that she was playing out a rather elaborate charade. She gestured with practised elegance and her speaking voice was the same cultured tone that I had heard on the phone.

I have always believed that in an occupation like mine, where you are visiting people's homes, clients must be accepted on face value and I endeavour to give all clients the same type of treatment and consideration without acting in a condescending manner or, more importantly, never embarrassing anyone. I was, at this time, struggling to gain some control and I was biting my cheek to stop myself bursting into hysterical laughter.

Just as I started to regain some discipline over myself, the lady's husband walked through the door, and it was time for another shock. The man stood well over six feet tall and had a thin, wiry build. His gaunt face was topped by a mop of rope-like white hair that needed a good combing, but the outstanding feature was the man's eyes—they bulged from their sockets and moved at an incredible rate as he looked me over; they shone with a zealous gleam which unnerved me somewhat.

The mood of hysterical laughter that I had previously felt was quickly replaced with a sense of foreboding that I had not felt since I was a small child, when my elder brother had subjected me to one of his many sessions of pleasure for him, and abject terror for me.

Mesmerised for the moment, I missed the name that was given to me as he introduced himself. The situation was getting more bizarre by the minute as the man continued talking and firing staccato bursts of questions at me—which he answered before I had the chance to utter a sound.

The man's wife was quite unaffected by the husband's behaviour and, in fact, joined in his questioning; however, she aimed the questions at him while I sat in the corner, stunned into silence by this couple's odd behaviour.

I decided to let him continue until they had made their respective points, and then try and restore some sanity to the situation; however, they continued their discussion unabated as I sat twiddling my thumbs. I thought that they would run out of steam, and I would be able to take control of the situation but, in fact, the opposite was the case. The woman continued her questioning of her husband, still framing her questions in her own precise manner. Without changing the pace or tone of her voice, her husband was now ranting and raving like a demented politician—spittle dribbling from the side of his mouth and running down his chin, eyes aflame with maniacal malice, and arms thrown about in gay abandon as he smashed his hands together to make a point or stamped his foot on the floor.

*Why me?* I thought, angry at myself for not identifying the woman as an oddball when she phoned. Then, determined to make the best of the situation, I ran through my mind possible courses of action that would either: let me do the job for which I had come; or exit from centre-stage with as little fuss as possible.

I thought over the alternatives. I could write off my time and effort and try to leave quietly while the couple were engrossed in their discussion, or maybe I should wait and see if the conversation subsided to somewhere near an average level and then ask questions and proceed as if nothing had happened. Then again, maybe I could do something bizarre—even more so than they were doing. *Yes,* that really appealed to me. I relaxed for the first time since I entered the house and let my mind run wild and wondered what I could do that would shock this eccentric duo.

It was only then that I noticed that the room was in a state of eerie quiet and the couple were looking at me as if I had blasphemed in church.

"Hey, I'm talking to you," the man said, then turned to his wife. "He's not taking any bloody notice, he's just sitting there with a stupid bloody smile on his face—as vacant as an empty block of land." He shook his head and continued: "You've picked a right one here, I can tell you."

I felt embarrassed and very much ill at ease having been caught in the act of trying to think of a way to turn the consultation back to my advantage. I was now caught off-guard and probably looked as odd to them as they had previously looked to me. I quickly collected my thoughts and tried to regain my composure before I answered.

"I wath justh." *Oh damn,* I thought, *why now?* I cursed the lisp that I occasionally lapsed into when I was extremely tired or stressed. I took a deep breath and concentrated on forming the words as I had been taught in speech therapy sessions, and this time I managed to get it right. "I was just thinking of your problem and the best way to solve it," I said in my most convincing manner, which had no impact on them at all, and left them unconvinced of my explanation.

"Well, you sure as hell better think of a way to solve our problem," the man said aggressively. "That's what you're here for—you're supposed to be an expert."

I ignored that barb and thought at least we should be able to get on with the consultation about their attacking dog, and then I could get the heck out of there.

Summoning up my most authoritative voice, I then explained how we would proceed. "I am going to ask you a question which I would like both of you to answer. The initial questions will be about the dog's behaviour."

Some sense of normalcy had been established so I proceeded. "Is the dog clean in the house?"

The lady answered first. "We have a slight problem with the dog's faeces from time to time, my dear," she stated.

Hiding a smile, I asked her husband would he agree with that. "Yeah," he said. "The little bastard craps all over the carpet." That sentence completed, the man regained his fanatical look and started ranting again. His eyes bulged and returned to focus on his wife who showed no response to the change of character and returned to her former behaviour and joined in their two-sided discussion and ignored me.

I sat in the corner feeling unwanted, unloved and unhappy, trying to fathom some sense in the whole episode. Then, just as I was about to try and say something about leaving, the man stood up and approached me, extending his hand. I stood up and accepted his handshake and he patted me on the shoulder warmly. "Well, you have been a great help. I'm glad we called you," he said. "We wouldn't have been able to solve the problem without you, would we?" he asked his wife. The wife nodded her head in agreement and handed me a monogrammed envelope containing my fee. "Yes, we are delighted that you came to help, and we really appreciate you altering your schedule to fit us in."

All this was said as I was ushered out the door, and goodbyes were offered with an invitation to drop in if I were ever in the area. Before I realised it, I was out the front door and walking past the poplars, wondering if I would ever have another case quite like this one. I had been paid for a consultation—which I never completed; I had given no advice and yet, I felt it was the hardest money I had ever earned, and I never got to see the dog!

# THE ATTACK-TRAINED DOG

ENQUIRIES REGARDING THE ATTACK TRAINING OF DOGS have brought about many amusing conversations on the phone. Giving an inexperienced person an attack-trained dog is like giving a child a loaded pistol to play with, so before I agree to even *test* a dog to see if it is suitable for this type of training, I always question the person enquiring as to the reason *why* they need an attack-trained dog.

Some of the answers I receive are incredible to say the least—even more so because the people are dead serious when questioned. Some typical examples are: "The next-door neighbour's a bloody mug, mate, a good bite on the bum might pull him into line a bit"; "I want the dog to bite my husband ... but only when he's drunk"; "I wanna dog to tear da froat out likona the TV a bigga black one"; "A bloke ripped me off in a dope deal and I want to fix him".

Then of course I get many serious enquiries from people who aren't sure of what they need. Most of the dogs are too young or not of a breed suitable for this type of work, but if they have good reason and a dog of suitable age and breed, the next step is to test the dog's temperament. And also check the people out to ensure that they're responsible and won't misuse the dog. Having said all that, and being experienced enough to pick out most of the fruitcakes, I still sometimes get caught, as the following story demonstrates.

A call came in from an ethnic gentleman who owned a milk bar and had been bashed twice by hoodlums misbehaving in his shop. He explained that he worked late, often on his own, and had large sums of cash on hand. He had a twenty-month-old German Shepherd who he had taken to obedience school, but had not shown any protective instincts. I agreed to test the dog and arranged to meet him at the local park to watch him work the dog through its obedience training, and then test the dog's temperament.

At the park he worked through its obedience routine without a problem, and the man showed he had excellent control over him. Before testing the dog, I explained what I was going to do, and the reaction I would require from the dog if we were to proceed with training.

The dog was a bit slow to react to agitation, but stood his ground, and when I approached him the second time in a suspicious manner, he reacted well. Once given the idea, the dog's response was strong, and he was a good candidate for the protective training course. I spent some time telling the client about the schedule of training and what I would expect from him, and gave him a detailed description of the training agenda—including the responsibility he would then undertake in owning a dog with attack-training experience.

All went well during this conversation and in fact he asked a lot of relevant questions and I had no doubt in my mind at this stage that he was a sensible person who would be responsible with his dog when it was trained. We agreed on a training date and I left for my next job.

Our next training session took place in the man's backyard. The dog underwent an agitation session which consisted of me approaching the dog, and then withdrawing when the dog responded in an aggressive manner. The session lasted for a period of about two minutes and the dog was left at the peak of his aggression; I told the man to release the dog and let it run free in the yard when I left.

It was at this time I got the first inkling that I may have misjudged the man. He complained about the length of time of the session, claiming it was too short. I explained that if I did any more the dog would go over its peak and the aggression may lessen, or the dog may treat the agitation as a game, or the dog may become frustrated with side effects, and patiently explained all the other associated problems. He remained firmly unconvinced, so I told him that if he doubted my ability to do the job, or if he was unhappy in any way, that we should terminate the training then, and he should take the dog to someone else. I went on to tell him that if he continued training, it would be as I had outlined in the program prior to commencement. There was definitely not to be *any* extra training sessions of agitation by friends in my absence, which may result in the dog becoming unpredictable. Finally, he agreed to my demands and seemed a little embarrassed that he had questioned me at all.

Another training session was completed a few days later without incident, and an appointment made for a third early in the next week.

The night before the session was due, the man rang and cancelled, telling me that his wife had been taken to hospital after collapsing at work. Approximately a week later he rang and made another appointment, for 2:00 p.m. the next day.

He met me at the front gate; I enquired about his wife's health and he said she was home from hospital and was weak, but making a slow recovery. He was telling me this as we walked down his driveway, and as we entered the yard I noticed the body of a woman lying against the wall of the garage. I ran towards the prone figure saying, "Your wife's collapsed!" While I was running, he tried to hold me back saying, "No, No, that's not her!" Well, I really didn't care if it was his wife, his sister, or whoever—the fact was, there was a body lying in an unusual position and obviously not well. The man was shouting now and becoming quite irate and then I realised why.

The figure was in fact a life-size dummy dressed in women's clothing, complete with an old wig.

Now it was my turn to become irate and I challenged the man over the use of the dummy. I accused him of using the dummy in training sessions—between my sessions. He agreed that he had, because he felt my sessions were too short and that he had used a friend to help him. I then asked who the clothing on the dummy belonged to and he said his wife. I couldn't believe it at first.

By agitating the dog with the dummy dressed in his wife's clothing he was building aggression which the dog would almost certainly associate with his wife because of the residual smell on her old clothing. This of course meant that the dog may well turn on his wife if the opportunity presented itself. I explained this to the man, who remained silent, and I continued on giving him the full blast and telling him he mustn't think much of his wife to place her in that situation. That accusation brought no response from him; I told him that I would not continue with any more training. I turned, preparing to leave.

At this moment his wife appeared at the back door—a small, slight woman dressed in black with an even blacker look on her face. She started screaming at her husband in their own language which of course I didn't understand; however, after some fourteen years of marriage myself and a veteran of many a tongue-lashing from my own wife, I didn't have to understand the language to realise the one-sided conversation that was taking place before me.

Believe me, I had heard it all before, maybe in a different language and certainly a lot quieter, but I had heard it all right. I stood, slightly embarrassed to be caught in the middle of a family row, especially when I didn't really know what had prompted her to let fly with such a tirade of abuse. This was the woman who had been rushed to hospital and was making a slow recovery, her husband had told me. I thought to myself, *if this lady is convalescing, she must be a handful when she is well.*

During her outburst the husband stood still, eyes downcast and completely submissive. Mind you, I didn't blame him for that, because she certainly intimidated me and she was screaming at him—not me. She continued her abuse, hardly stopping to take a breath, her voice rising and falling to emphasise a point, and her hands slapping together or against her head with almost uncontrolled violence. During the course of my home training, I have sat in on many pretty good family arguments, but I had never seen anything like this. My own wife's ability to nag paled into insignificance beside this woman. What amazed me was her husband's attitude. The man had been a brash, cocky type when I was irate with him over the use of the dummy only moments before, but now he was reduced to a meek, mild shadow of the man he had seemed.

I had been almost hypnotised by the scene before me, and now I looked back to the woman. Her face had turned a dark shade, and the veins stood out on her temples as she finished her last torrent of abuse. She was standing on the back steps of the house some three feet above our heads, hands on hips, then turned towards me.

Well, I have never made any false claims of being any sort of a hero, and at this point, retreat and a fast exit seemed like a great idea. I made a fast U-turn and headed for the gate, which was about ten feet away; however, I only managed about one step before her voice rang out in broken but quite understandable English.

"Hey, where you go, big-shot dog trainer? I gonna talka to you, fella." *Like hell*, I thought. I cop heaps at home, and I was damn sure I wasn't going to cop more because she was angry with her husband. I'm no mug when it comes to summing up losing situations, and this was a certain no-win, so I reached the gate in double-quick time and headed for my bike. As I disappeared down the driveway the lady's voice was ringing in my ears and believe me, it seemed to get louder as I moved away.

As I unhooked my crash helmet and prepared to leave, the husband, who had followed me out the drive, thankfully on his own, his wife having slammed the door and gone inside, still screaming and carrying on, approached me, apologising for his wife's behaviour. "What was she upset with me for?" I asked. "I haven't even met her." The man looked rather sheepish and told me that she had seen the dummy being used to agitate the dog and objected to the use of her clothes, and not being slow to link the dog's aggression and her scent on the clothes and the possible result had given her husband a large helping of abuse.

He wilted under the pressure and used me for an excuse, telling her it was my idea, hence her anger at me. Well, I wasn't at all impressed by what he had told her, but I could sympathise with him as, put in the same position, I would have ratted on my best friend to quieten down the harridan he had married. Given the information, I now understood his wife's aggression towards me and I could see no reason for further conversation, so I kicked over the bike and headed off into the sunset.

Like all husbands, I often think I am hard done by by my wife, but after witnessing that exhibition I realised that of course I am *spoilt* at home. Being married to that lady must be the absolute pits, and thinking back on the incident I wonder if I had unwittingly nearly contributed to aiding and abetting in a bizarre type of revenge…

# LISA THE LION CUB

IN MY PROFESSIONAL LIFE AS A DOG TRAINER, I have been fortunate over the years to train many different breeds of dogs—mostly the common breeds, and occasionally one of the rarer breeds.

I have always been interested in expanding my knowledge of animal training and have read many books and taken a keen interest either by means of television or live performances on methods used by other trainers, and on any type of animal.

Naturally enough, I was keen to try out my own ideas of training a type of animal other than a canine, and I was given a rare opportunity to do *just* that some years ago. It produced some amusing incidents that I will relate here.

One morning, the owner of a small travelling circus arrived at my training kennels with two lion cubs. The circus was running short of money, and the owner wanted the cubs boarded and given some basic training so that they could be handled.

Of course, I jumped at the opportunity and the cubs were soon settled in a large unused aviary that was perfect for their accommodation. The initial agreement was that the cubs would be boarded for two weeks, but it turned out to be closer to three months.

I did not know anything about the nutritional requirements of lions, and I suspected that the owner knew even less, so I organised a visit from a vet who was familiar with lions. The cubs were checked over and wormed and armed with my newfound knowledge of how to care and maintain a lion, I proceeded to initiate some training sessions.

My wife has put up with many situations since our marriage, and she just shook her head and smiled when I burst through the door, as excited as a child on Christmas morning, explaining that I had an unusual booking.

Most ladies would take the sight of two lion cubs in their backyard with some hesitation and trepidation, but my wife took it as all in a day's work, and made no objection.

My father was a different story. He had visions of his grandchildren being eaten and he was not amused. My parents were booked to travel overseas to visit my sister, and Dad decided to cancel the trip—unless I got rid of the cubs. My father, a dour Scotsman, stood firmly unconvinced by my arguments that they were only cubs and still playful.

My mum was a very gentle lady, and was much more tactful than my dad, and indeed a lot less vocal. She set about laying the groundwork for the lions to be returned to the circus, in that quiet, determined way that mothers have.

Mum was just as unhappy about the situation as my dad, but canny enough to know that a direct confrontation may not get the result they both wanted: the cubs as far away from their grandchildren as possible.

Well, of course, I just couldn't understand what all the fuss was about! Here I was, with the best thing that had ever happened to me at work, and some people could not appreciate my good fortune.

The training started well, and I introduced some light handling methods as I believed that the cubs would respond more to them than to the heavy, compulsive techniques that are normally associated with the training of lions.

It was soon evident that the male had retained all his basic instincts of survival, and he soon became a problem. He overcame his initial inhibitions and became territorial in the aviary. After only two or three sessions, I realised that he would not respond to my methods. He was bad-tempered, moody and a downright sneak, who would circle behind and then lash out without warning.

On the other hand, the female (whom I had named Lisa) was consistent in her mood, good-natured and receptive to training. She seemed to have no vices and was a delight to be around. She was like an overgrown housecat and would stalk me and jump up in a playful mood when given the opportunity.

Within a week, she was walking beside me and was content to exercise on a twenty-foot lead in the training compound. I ceased training the male and we came to an understanding where he would let me partition him off, and clean out his area and feed him. He would ignore me at all other times. Lisa and the male bonded well together and played for hours in normal litter activities.

Lisa and I were developing an unusual bond (much to the dismay of my father) and both cubs were growing at an amazing rate.

After three months, I thought that the circus must have gone broke, as I had not had any word from the day they left the cubs. Then, without announcement and no apology, the owner turned up, paid his bill, loaded the cubs into a cage and left within minutes, leaving me annoyed and feeling cheated (and my father and the neighbours delighted).

Although we lived on a five-acre block, the neighbours never did get used to the sight of Lisa and I walking around the property. The fact that Lisa was on a lead and under control did little to ease their doubts.

I thought I had seen the last of the cubs and went about my business training the less exotic animals that were normally at the kennels. Dogs.

Eight or nine months later, the circus owner returned with Lisa and requested boarding for a week. The male had been sent to a lion park, as he had proved difficult to handle. Lisa had maintained all of her charm, and we had a happy reunion. She had trebled her size since I first saw her, and while she had not yet reached maturity, she was a *big cat* and an awesome sight up close.

Lisa and I quickly settled back into our routine, and we were soon walking around the property, and anyone could approach her and pat her without objection on her part. She was one big docile, happy cat.

One afternoon as I was finishing my kennel rounds, an old friend of mine arrived with his wife, who knew all about Lisa—but Ted knew nothing about our unusual feline guest.

Ted is a big man, about six feet five inches in his socks. He and I had attended the same high school and later were stationed together when I was in the police force. While I had opted out of the job to set up my training kennels, Ted had stayed in the police and made a successful career for himself.

I greeted them in the office and then excused myself and left them talking to my wife, while I finished off my kennel rounds.

As I left the kennels, I decided to bring Lisa up with me. I was always quick to show off the cuddly cub, so I hitched a lead onto a twenty-foot lead and walked up to the office.

As I turned the corner, Ted was standing with his back to me, engrossed in conversation. While the two women saw me approaching with Lisa strolling beside me, neither woman acknowledged the cub as we approached.

I tied Lisa to a pole, allowing her some freedom, and she followed me slowly, stopping to have a roll in the grass on the way. Ted was still oblivious of Lisa's presence, and as I neared him the phone in the house rang.

As I passed Ted on the way to answer the phone, I handed him the middle section of the lead, requesting him to, "Hold this for a minute, mate." Ted didn't look up but kept on talking as he took the lead, without comment.

My phone call had to be cut short as I could not hear what was being said. I walked out to find the two women almost paralytic with laughter, due to the antics of Lisa and the response from the hapless Ted.

Lisa had taken an instant liking to the big man and had wrapped her lead around his legs several times, effectively immobilising him as she purred contentedly, and rubbed herself up against Ted's legs.

Ted stood as if sculptured in marble, a look of stunned terror etched on his granite features. Ted, the veteran of fifteen years of police service, a half a dozen Bathurst Easter weekend bike riots and the Vietnam Moratorium Day marches, was neatly wrapped and completely intimidated by Lisa, a gentle lion cub.

Ted was not the least bit impressed by Lisa's affection for him, and to this day will not believe that I did not set up the confrontation. Being a close friend, I have made it my duty to relay the story to every policeman I have met since over the years. The tale of Ted in the lion's den has become legendary within the Force.

Lisa only stayed with me a short time on her second visit, and I arranged to deliver her back to the circus which was playing at a suburban location on the weekend.

Early on the morning I was to deliver Lisa, I had a phone call from a friend of mine, who at the time was the current Australian World Cup soccer team goalkeeper. He was conducting a junior coaching session that morning and asked whether I was available to help him with the coaching. The park at which the session was to be held was near where I had to drop Lisa, so I readily agreed and arranged to pick him up.

I secured Lisa in the rear of my panel van with a lead, and she settled down and was soon asleep. I forgot about her as I drove through the heavy weekend traffic.

I pulled up outside my friend's place and sounded the horn, and glanced over my shoulder to check Lisa, who was still asleep. My friend jumped into the car and we discussed the training he had done in preparation for an important club match the next day.

At this stage, Lisa and my friend were both oblivious of each other as we motored down the highway. As we neared Parramatta, I noticed some movement in the rear of the van. There was no division between Lisa and us, and as I watched in the rear-vision mirror, she stood up and stretched in the slinky manner that only felines can show.

As she stretched, it occurred to me that I had not seen her in a confined space before. She looked huge; in fact, she seemed to take up all the rear of the van.

At this moment, my friend noticed the movement in the rear, and knowing that I often carried dogs, made the comment that the dog, in fact, "smelt funny". Lisa chose this moment to let out a full-throated roar of greeting, which was magnified many times in the confined area of my panel van.

My friend's reflexes showed why he was the country's number one goalkeeper. He took one hurried glance over his shoulder, opened the door and readied himself for a jump to safety. The fact that we were travelling at 80 km/h did not deter him one *bit*—as he had obviously decided that the jump was safer than the ride!

I grabbed his arm and as I pulled over to the kerb, I tried to explain that she was only a cub, and that he was in no danger. He told me what he thought of me in the best Australian tradition, and even after being introduced to Lisa, remained firmly unconvinced about his safety. I had as much trouble getting him back into the van as a person trying to load a fractious stallion onto a horse float! Finally, he wedged himself into the corner of the van and did not take his eyes off Lisa for the remainder of the trip ... he didn't say much either.

Lisa, by this time, had lost interest in the proceedings, and had gone back to sleep.

The remainder of the trip to the circus went without incident, but the next day my friend's team was beaten by four goals in what was expected to be a close game. He blamed me; said he had a nightmare match because his nerves were shot to pieces.

Lisa didn't stay long with the circus, and was released into the Lion Park with her own kind, but I still have fond memories of our partnership. She and I had a lot in common...both misunderstood!

## LISA THE LION CUB

Lisa was a lion cub
A pretty cub was she
Although she really was quite tame
My friends did not agree
I used to take her for a walk

She'd stroll along at ease
While neighbours fled in panic
I could tell they weren't too pleased
My father got quite angry,
He said I was insane
He said, "She'll eat my grandkids"
And I would be to blame
A friend who came to visit me
Was quickly introduced
And Lisa loved him thoroughly
My friend was not amused
Now I don't know what the fuss was
She really was quite tame
She used to growl and hiss sometimes
But it was just a game
In my panel van one day
She scared a friend of mine
He said, "Behind bars you both should be
and for a long, long time!"
Now this tale ends happily
As every story should
Lisa's in a lion park
With others of her brood.

# PARK CONFRONTATION

THIS CASE HISTORY INVOLVES A SIX-MONTH-OLD ENGLISH SPRINGER SPANIEL bitch who had been imported from England and had just been released from quarantine. The owner was an experienced breeder herself, with many years of show judging and exhibiting behind her.

After the dog was released from the quarantine kennels, her behaviour was erratic and she overreacted to almost any noise, and any visitor to the house, and also to the other dogs owned by the breeder.

I was contacted to help, and attended the owner's home where the problem was discussed at length during which time I was observing the dog's behaviour. During the conversation with the owner, I noticed that she was an excitable person herself, and that the activity in the house bordered on chaotic. In fact, as time passed, I later referred to the place as 'Chaos Castle'. Phones rang continuously, people arrived at the door, and many other distractions took place during the consultation. The owner, a lady of tremendous enthusiasm and energy, took all of this in her stride, hurrying from one interruption to another and then returning to continue the consultation before the next inevitable interruption.

I wanted to observe the dog's reactions outside the house so I suggested a walk down to the park. The dog threw herself down on the ground and whimpered when the lead was produced; however, she settled down quickly when handled firmly. So we set out to the park accompanied by the owner.

On the way to the park, I explained the importance of quiet, firm handling and the fact

that any situation which was stressful to the dog would slow down our progress. The dog continued to strain on the lead until we reached the park where I attached a ten-metre exercise lead. She showed a lack of confidence, however, and would not venture more than two or three feet away from us.

The park was quite large and I noticed a small dog running loose with its owners at the other end, about a hundred yards away. As I did not want any confrontation with another dog at this stage, we stayed up our own end, and I continued to walk the dog, giving her time to adjust to the new surroundings. For the next ten minutes I walked the dog and, unnoticed by me, the dog from the other end had approached and was bearing down on us—tail raised and looking for trouble! At this stage, the owners—an elderly lady, a younger woman and her son—were well behind and obviously unconcerned with their dog's behaviour.

A warning growl as the dog charged was my first indication that the dog had approached, and my first reaction was to protect my pupil, so I hastily put myself between the two. This was no deterrent to the snapping Terrier who spun around and launched himself at the Springer pup, who, restrained by the leash, was fighting to get behind me. I called out to the owner to put her dog on a lead and she replied that she didn't have one and that her dog didn't need a lead. The dog, oblivious to our conversation, renewed its attack with increased ferocity and had almost made contact with my charge when I pushed him aside with my foot.

Then, all hell broke loose. The owner of the dog sprinted towards me with a murderous look on her face. I have often said that dogs mimic their owners, and in this case, it was true. The aggressive performance of her dog paled in comparison to the owner, who showed all the characteristics of a well-trained attack dog. With pupils dilated, nostrils flaring and blood pressure rising, she descended upon me and accused me of kicking her puppy. The dog by this stage had continued his harassment, switching his attacks between my pupil and myself—without preference for either.

The breeder, until this time, had remained quiet, as all this action took only a few seconds.

Above the noise, I tried to explain to the owner of the Terrier that I had not kicked her dog but merely pushed it away, and *repeated* my request to control her dog—as I did not want either myself or my dog bitten. Any attempt at reasoning with the woman was useless, as she continued her abuse without seeming to draw a breath. The situation was growing worse by the second with the Spaniel now yelping with fear and wrapping its lead around my legs, me fighting to gain control of the dog, and my composure and the woman's abuse stimulating *her* dog onto greater efforts.

Aided by the confusion, her dog made another attempt to attack the Spaniel and I pushed it away *again* with my foot. This triggered the woman into more action and she charged in with even more murderous intent. Then, just as would happen in any good storybook, where the good guys are rescued just when all seems lost, the breeder stepped in between us, spreading her arms out to shield the dog and myself, and stopping the woman in her tracks.

As surprised as I was by this action, I was even more surprised when my heroine of the moment berated the woman with a stream of the bluest language imaginable! *Well,* I thought, *this will shock her,* after all it had shocked *me.* However, I had underestimated our assailant, who showed that she, too, could use her own inimitable style of Aussie profanities with consummate skill. Now I was placed in another dilemma—should I break in and try to reason? Or should I take the Spaniel to safety?

I did not lack experience in violent situations, having worked for many years as a bouncer at pubs and dances, and I had always prided myself on the ability to talk sense into the most aggressive patrons, or to stand my ground and handle a problem physically—if there was no other way.

I must admit, however, that I had never faced a violent *female* before, and so after examining the alternatives, I decided that the breeder was more than a match for the lady and her dog, and the Spaniel and I headed for safety, both with our tails between our legs.

# 'CUTIE'

Devastation! That was the only way I could describe the scene before me. I was standing in the middle of what *had* been a well-laid-out and lovingly cared for suburban backyard. Now it was littered with all kinds of debris, ranging from expensive plants and shrubs to pieces of the plastic and stone garden pots which had once graced the garden.

Holes of various sizes and depth were also prominent, and what had been a very expensive garden setting resembled the type of kindling wood ideal for the Sunday barbecue.

Standing beside me was the owner of the house—a man of such size, girth and manner not to be taken lightly. However, now he stood and surveyed the damage to his garden, his former pride and joy, with a defeated attitude—the type of attitude that I had seen before when a sportsman had been beaten into submission by an adversary of superior ability.

At this moment, the perpetrator of the carnage burst onto the scene—with all the vibrant energy and undisguised glee of a playground full of children who had just broken up for school holidays.

Showing no remorse for the damage done to the garden or the stress caused to his master, the six-month-old Labrador pup launched himself at us from about six feet. His owner showed amazing agility for a man of his size. He deftly side-stepped the onrushing dog and headed for the safety of the house.

Once inside, with the dog now unleashing a virtual torrent of barking, he turned to me with a look of total exasperation and said, "What can I do? I have given him the best of everything: a good home, he's well fed, we walk him, we groom him, we play with him and all we get in return is problems every day. He chews, he digs, he barks, he howls and to make it worse—he's happy the whole time."

At this point the owner walked over to the side window of the room and motioned for me to follow. "Look," he said, indicating a hole of mammoth proportions. "What do you think of that?" I hesitated to answer, wondering whether I should look suitably impressed, or maybe try and ease the situation with a comical remark.

The thought crossed my mind that the Department of Main Roads may be able to harness the dog's energy and utilise him to dig trenches! However, the harassed owner was obviously looking to me as his last hope, and I decided a frivolous remark would be inappropriate at this time.

I suggested that we sit down and discuss the dog's problems and complete an information sheet on the dog's habits. During the discussion that followed, I learned that the dog had been purchased on impulse, without previous thought or preparation.

I then asked for the dog's name and the owner replied, "Cutie." *You must be joking*, I thought. Fancy naming a big, virile, boisterous dog—Cutie. No wonder he's rebelling!

We went through the normal profile on the dog's behaviour with the owner's exasperation growing by the minute. Cigarettes were lit, smoked and stamped out in quick succession as the story of man and dog unfolded.

The sheet completed I then asked to see the dog's pedigree papers and the man produced them from a neat folder which contained all the relevant vaccination papers as well. While I was studying the pedigree the ultimate irony of the situation was revealed.

Pedigree papers are filled out giving the kennel name prior to the name of each given name of a dog. The dog's given name was not "Cutie", as called by his owner, but "Q.T.", which had been shortened from Quiet Time.[1]

-----

1   The dog in this case was very receptive to training and the owner proved a capable handler, and owner and dog are living *happily ever after* in a neat, orderly suburban house.

# TALL TALES

IN MY DAYS WORKING AS A DOG TRAINER, I have been told *many* tall tales, with the storytellers always able to confirm the validity of their story, and ever ready to swear to the *truth* of the matter.

Several have stuck in my mind. Here they are:

The storyteller in this case was an old bushie of indeterminate age. His wrinkled face attested to a few score years under the outback sun, and his hands, now wrinkled with age, still showed signs of the strength that many years of hard work had given them.

He sat back in his chair, rolled a cigarette from the makings on his lap and reflected on days gone by; then, with a twinkle in his eye, he relayed his tale.

"Talk about fleas—I've seen them so big outback that the bull ants were terrified of them. Big and brown they were, and could jump five feet at a hop. We've had all sorts of plagues outback: locusts, mice, kangaroos and flies—but nothing to match the flea plague of '71."

He licked the paper down on his cigarette and cast an expert eye over the shape of his rollie before nodding his head in approval and poking in the ends.

"Yeah, that was bad all right. Poor bloody dogs suffered, I can tell you. Poor buggers would be working the sheep and tuckered out from the extra weight they were carrying."

He gestured at me with the unlit smoke and then paused for effect. "Believe me, son, we tried everything—the vet, the chemist—*no one* could give us *anything* that was worth a bloody *thing*. The bloody dogs had scratched themselves raw—bleeding some of them were. Well, we called in the bigwigs from the university, and then the research blokes arrived. Some of them had so many letters after their names you couldn't have jumped a workhorse over them."

He finally lit his cigarette, inhaled and savoured the taste of the tobacco. "Needles, pastes, rinses—they tried, but the fleas were *still* there, long after they all buggered off home.

"You wouldn't believe it—one of the locals worked out a way to beat them. All the bloody educated experts—and young Blue from out at the Brown farm found the way!

"He wasn't considered too bright, this kid—they reckoned he was the only kid ever to go to the local primary who had failed play lunch. Anyway, he was watching his dog in the river one day and noticed that the fleas didn't like the water too much, so he hit upon an idea."

I fidgeted a little in my seat as the story dragged on, but he continued: "What he did was build a fire on one side of the river then he took his dogs back to the other side. One at a time he swam them across the river, each one of them holding a big stick in its mouth. As the dogs swam over, the fleas all jumped onto the stick to keep dry, then when they reached the other side he threw the stick covered in the fleas into the fire. Bit unorthodox, but it worked …" He smiled wryly then continued:

"Then there was the time …"

# THE AUSTRALIAN STING

IT WAS A BEAUTIFUL SUMMER'S DAY—a light breeze played across the water as I sat eating my lunch on the harbour foreshore of Sydney's most elite suburb.

My first three jobs of the day had gone well, and now, after having lunch in such pleasant surroundings, I was about to start a new job, around the corner from my lunch spot.

I gathered up my rubbish and headed for the bin nearby, at the same time going over in my mind what I knew of the new client. The lady was recommended by a former client of mine. She owned a six-month-old Australian Terrier which refused to walk on a lead and continually soiled in the house.

I gathered my training gear and consultation book and walked around the corner to the house.

The houses in the area were of roughly the same era although their design differed greatly and some had been modernised. Most were impressive in size, and the street gave the impression of old-world charm and old money. The people living here were mainly the descendants of the true business pioneers in Australia—families that had made good early and built upon their capital and consolidated their family wealth.

The house that I entered had impressive grounds with a multitude of trees and gardens set out, and was cared for in a loving manner. An old gardener kneeled in the shade, patiently tending a colourful rose bush. He returned my greeting with a nod of his head then dutifully returned to his pruning.

As I walked up the front steps, I cast my eyes over the huge front doors set back inside a sandstone archway. It resembled the type of entrance seen in the old castles of England. The doors were supported by three huge brass hinges on either side, and an ornamental door-knocker—the size of a man's hand—announced my arrival. My two knocks echoed throughout the house making me wince at my own heavy-handedness.

I waited quietly outside as the echoes of the door knocks died in my ears, and I heard footsteps approaching. The door was opened silently by an attractive lady in her forties who eyed me up and down as I introduced myself and handed her my business card.

The way she looked me over was my first inkling that she was unhappy, and her following remarks confirmed my thoughts.

"Mr Fraser, whenever you have a training appointment at this residence you shall enter through the tradesman's entrance at the side, and never through the front entrance. The passage is at the side of the house and I will meet you there presently," she added. Having said that, she closed the door in my face and left me standing, staring at the brass door-knocker.

My pleasant mood was shattered; I stood there for a moment gathering my thoughts before I turned and walked down the driveway, past the still kneeling gardener.

"Leaving already?" he enquired with a wry smile upon his face.

"Yes," I replied. "The lady doesn't want her dog trained after all!"

As I walked back to my bike I thought back over the conversation. It wasn't *what* was said, but the *way* it was said, and the manner in which the lady(?) acted.

I now had a couple of hours to kill before my next appointment so I called in to see a vet friend of mine in the area, and she had a good laugh as I pantomimed the incident and related the story.

I arrived home that night after another two uneventful lessons, and after making my normal phone calls regarding the business, I sat down with a cup of tea and the nightly papers. The phone rang before I had finished my cuppa and a familiar voice echoed down the line:

"Mr Fraser," and the lady went on to identify herself. "I take it by your exit from our lesson this morning that you took offence at what I said."

"Yes, you're right," I replied. "Not only did I take offence at *what* you said but also the *manner* in which you acted, and the *tone* that you used."

"Well, you must understand—"

I cut in over the top of her conversation. "I understand many things. I train dogs for people from all walks of life and from all over Sydney, from the working-class areas, the so-called under-privileged areas, through to the area in which you live. In fact, I have trained dogs for, and become friends with, many of the people in your street—one being the person who recommended my services to you   and during the twelve years that I have been training dogs in these lessons, I have never once been asked to use a side door, or been addressed so rudely and in such a manner—and I can assure you that I was certainly offended."

"Mr Fraser, I think that you have overreacted to this situation; however, as you have come highly recommended I will overlook your attitude and we shall make another appointment!"

I hesitated before answering, careful to delete any 'language' from my reply. "I don't think you understand. You and I are *not* going to get along together, and I will *not* be training your dog. I am afraid we live in different worlds, and from your manner with me this afternoon, you should be living in the eighteenth century, when the type of class distinction you favour was prevalent and accepted."

There was a distinct pause before she answered; I waited for her reply, counselling my mood so I could be as rational as possible, something that I certainly didn't *feel*.

"Well, Mr Fraser," she continued confidently. "You don't know me, but I *always* get what I want in the end, and I can assure you that you *will* train my dog for me."

Her manner was growing more irritating by the minute, and I decided that it was time that this conversation was finished. "It will be a cold day in hell before I work for you in any capacity. Now, I don't wish to be as rude to you now as you were to me today, but I am busy so I am going to hang up now," I said, barely able to control my anger.

"Mr Fraser, remember what I said …"

The phone went dead in my hand and I went back to my paper, annoyed that she had *again* had the last word.

Several weeks went by, and I had almost forgotten about the incident 'till I had reason to go back to the same street in which that lady lived. It was to visit, in fact, the lady who had recommended me to her, who was her close friend as well as neighbour.

After working her dog and sitting over tea and cake I was asked about the incident with her friend. I explained what had happened and my client was in fits of laughter throughout the story.

"Well, that's *exactly* the way she is. Take her or leave her, but she really is a very nice person and a good friend; however, I can see that you two are not likely to get on at all."

I shook my head. "Well, I'll leave her. She may have good qualities, but I certainly didn't see them."

I finished my tea and left for my next lesson. As I pulled up at the lights at the bottom end of the street, I noticed a Mercedes Sports Car, some twenty-five years old and in pristine condition, beside me. I looked the car over, enviously admiring gleaming paintwork and classic lines.

The driver of the car then beeped the horn lightly to attract my attention and waved, giving me a smile. I waved back and smiled, trying to identify the pretty face behind the dark sunglasses. The lady driver then pulled her sunglasses down from one ear and smiled cheekily.

It was my rude lady friend from up the street!

Before I recovered from this impudence the lights changed and she dropped the clutch of the car. The motor responded with a throaty roar, leaving me with the screaming sound of red-hot tyres in my ears and egg on my face once again. Score three to the lady.

Months went by and during this time I had three jobs from clients in the area, all recommended from the cheeky lady in the Mercedes; however, my feelings towards her did not soften one bit. Several times I thought over the incident, and each time I felt that I had been skilfully put down.

One afternoon, I was finishing my last lesson with a young woman in the eastern suburbs. She owned an Australian Terrier, and I was pleased with the results of the sessions. We were sitting, talking over the exercises, when the doorbell rang. The lady who owned the dog left to answer the call while I sat and collected my paperwork.

I was picking up a paper from the floor when the lady entered, followed by her visitor, whom she introduced as her mother. I stood up to meet the lady and was completely taken by surprise when her mum turned out to be my former antagonist.

She now stood before me, smiling sweetly with her hand outstretched in greeting. "Mr Fraser, how nice to see you again. I wish to thank you for training my dog—even if it was by proxy."

I stood, dumbfounded. I had been ghosted skilfully and neatly, and her words returned to me. "You don't know me but I always get what I want and I assure you, you will train my dog." I felt angry and used. I looked to her daughter who had taken part in the conspiracy and she returned my look, a little embarrassed. I looked back to the lady, who stood there self-assured with her hand still outstretched and still smiling sweetly as if oblivious to my hesitation.

The situation eased almost immediately as I held out my hand, determined not to be a sore loser, and I smiled back at the lady.

"Well," I said with a sigh. "I guess that makes it 4/0 to you. I have been conned by a true artist in classic style."

"Don't feel bad about it," her daughter piped in. "Mum has conned Dad, parliamentarians, leading businessmen and even a visiting royal into getting her own way, so at least you are in good company."

We sat down to tea and scones, but somehow I had lost my appetite, and the lady was so polite I almost preferred her when she was rude!

Maybe I *was* a poor loser?!

🐾
🐾

# THE SUNDAY LIST

SUNDAY MORNING. IT WAS A BRIGHT SUNNY DAY and I was relaxing over my second pot of tea, the Sunday papers spread out in disarray on the table. I had read most of the papers and was contemplating on what to do with the rest of the day, when my wife entered the room and I was brought back to the painstaking reality of what I would *really* do with my Sunday.

It was a Sunday morning ritual that had been played out nearly every Sunday since our marriage fifteen years ago. My wife would, without fail, produce a work list. This was made up of all the jobs that she deemed necessary to do that day. Sometimes the list was a little daunting; in fact, sometimes the list was so *long,* a show-jumping horse would have had trouble clearing it.

The 'Sunday List' had been the butt of many jokes over the years, mainly between my brother-in-law and myself, but my wife showed a remarkable lack of humour over her List. Every Sunday the List was presented with the serious kind of attitude that the Federal Treasurer assumes when he brings down his yearly budget!

It seems my wife can't stand the thought of me being idle on a Sunday. I would be quite happy to while the hours away in front of the television, or any other such diversion that required little or no effort.

One Sunday in winter, it rained steadily throughout the day, and any thought of working outdoors was out of the question. My List for the day had several indoor jobs that I quickly completed and I thought myself free for the day. Motorcycle races were being televised live, and I lay back on the lounge covered by a blanket and basked in my freedom.

My wife wore a track between the kitchen and the lounge room, always in front of the television where I lay in a blissfully relaxed state. It was obvious my wife was searching for something else to add to the List and thus interrupt my bliss. Our confrontations over the List were not in any way serious, and in most cases my arguments as to the *contents* of the List were given and received in good-natured banter.

I thought any addition to the List at this stage was outside the rules, and the accepted attitude we shared to the List, and I made the mistake of stating this before my wife had found a job that could be completed outside—but under the shelter of the carport. We had recently purchased flyscreens in kit form, and two windows were under shelter.

Now, the bike race was at a critical stage, and I was quite warm, and the thought of missing the exciting finish to the race and standing in a draughty old carport did not appeal to me. I feel that I am at my best under pressure, and I came up with an excuse off the top of my head that even I was proud of.

"I can't do it! It's over five feet, and needs a council permit." Now my wife is not slow to pick up on any form of indiscretion on my part, and knows that I am prepared to stretch the truth at times, especially if it is to avoid an item on the List.

She stood and looked at me, unsure of my sincerity, while I lay back, trying my best to look earnest. Owner-builders now were required by law to pay a fee for any work done on their property over a certain cost, and my wife and I had participated in a conversation recently on the subject with friends of ours. I could almost see her mind working overtime as she reflected on the conversation. "You know what the neighbours are like, they would dob me in."

I could feel her weaken, and she walked out of the room muttering about councils while I settled back down under the blankets, warmed further by my temporary victory.

My victory and feeling of wellbeing, my comfort and my bike race—all exited the stage when my brother-in-law turned up. His sole purpose in life, it seems, is to cause me trouble, and when my wife commented about the council regulations, he not only blew my excuse, he also made my wife feel foolish at her gullibility.

So, I was soon out under the carport, fitting screens, while my wife and brother-in-law sat inside, drinking tea and eating my cake. My brother-in-law, being the thoughtful, good bloke that he is, did call out the name of the rider who won the race.

So, the traditional Sunday List was presented each Sunday, and after my indiscretion over the council permit, no excuses were accepted. Not once in all these years had I nearly achieved completing *all* the items listed, and still my wife, to her credit, would the next week dutifully complete her List and present it, along with sundry instructions, on the next Sunday.

I had learnt from bitter experience that it was easier to at least *try* to complete the set tasks than to argue, or try to find some excuse to leave the List till next week.

Sitting at the table, I scanned this week's List. The first item on the List was to clear out the wood beside the barbecue. As summer was approaching and the risk of spiders increased, I felt that this was for the safety of the children, and for once my wife and I agreed on one item of the List, at least.

I donned a pair of heavy work gloves, placed my wheelbarrow beside the pile of wood and set about my task. The wood was all light kindling, and in no time at all, I was down to the bottom of the pile. The wood had soaked up a lot of moisture, and I was startled when a frog jumped out of the pile looking for a safe area. My son was in the backyard playing with our dog, and I called out to him, telling him I had found a frog.

My son is ten years old, and has a talent with animals of all types, breeds and sizes that never fails to amaze and delight me. His strong and gentle attitude has a calming effect on animals and small children, and he attracts them all. The garden is his jungle, and it abounds with all types of lizards, insects and birds that attract and hold his attention for hours.

The frog was quickly captured and an esky home was made, partially filled with water, rocks and greenery. A lid was added and holes pierced for ventilation. Proud of his work, my son invited me to inspect the frog's elaborate home, and I approved on the condition that he did not regard the home as permanent, and a two-day limit was agreed to.

The day marched on, and I wore out *long* before the List had been completed, and I forgot all about the frog. During the latter part of the week while working in the garage, I noticed the esky was still in place, and that fresh greenery was hanging from the side of the lid. On inspection, I found that the frog was still alive in its unusual home, which had even more refinements added.

I was angry with my son. He had breached our agreement. The frog had been confined for too long in my view. I entered the house and found my son watching television, and I confronted him with my find. I demanded an explanation. He had read up on frogs, he informed me, and had provided shelter and a suitable diet and even exercised the frog each day by playing with it. In his own eyes he had provided all that was necessary. The thought that the frog may be *unhappy* about its confinement had not occurred to him.

Still my anger remained. I reminded him of our agreement. For the next ten minutes I gave him my reasons for accusing him of thoughtlessness. It was not natural for the frog to be confined. The frog had no activity. It could not regulate its position in accordance with temperatures. How did he know that the flies he was catching and giving to the frog were enough to sustain him or her? My son sat wide-eyed as I ran through the list. I finished by asking him how he would like to be cooped up in four walls day after day, with no escape and no variation in routine. I walked from the room, leaving the decision regarding the frog's freedom weighing heavily on my son's shoulders, and sat in the kitchen with my wife, who had overheard the conversation. "I can't believe it," I said. "He should know better than that."

My wife stared at me for a long moment then said very quietly with a touch of exasperation that hung uneasily on my conscience, "You know, I feel just like that frog, boxed in day after day, looking at four walls—trapped." I looked for a touch of humour in her eyes, a hint of a smile, but there was none. She was deadly serious. The contents of my conversation and accusations to my son flashed through my mind.

How many times had I heard my wife express her feelings of frustration—the housework, the same schedule repeated day in, day out, being tied to the house to answer our business phone, boxed in day after day. She had left the obvious question hanging, unspoken, but *present* all the same.

*Did I care more about the freedom of a garden frog or my wife's happiness?*

The frog and my wife were liberated that day, and now enjoy their respective freedoms. Life goes on the same for me, still shackled on Sundays, condemned forever to a life sentence of Sunday Lists, with absolutely no time off for good behaviour.

# THE SUNDAY LIST

Sunday morning half asleep
Scratch my head and stretch my feet
Read the papers, drink some tea
Sitting there contentedly
Then my wife enters the room
And I feel impending doom
She reads out the day's work intended
My Sunday rest is now ended
I plead—This is the day of rest
But my wife is not impressed
There're things to paint and lawns to mow
Then the garden you can hoe
Sometimes I claim that I'm not well
And I need a little spell
But my pleas fall on deaf ears
Even if I cry real tears
A husbands' union there should be
For poor overworked guys just like me
Stop work meetings demarcation
Every Sunday a vacation
But it seems that I'm condemned
To mow and paint and weed and mend
Every Sunday of my life
Watched over by my loving wife.

# DOCTOR DEATH

MY CLIENTS WHO BOOK IN TO HAVE THEIR DOG'S OBEDIENCE TRAINED are offered a course of six lessons, which are given once a week over a six-week period. Cancellations during the course are common, and excuses for cancellations range from the plausible to the ridiculous. Family illness and business commitments are common.

It is obvious that some people do not wish to continue with the course. Some people book in on impulse, and then realise that they must work between lessons to achieve a result. Even though this is explained to all clients before they start, they lose interest when the initial novelty wears off. Others get the result they want before the course is completed, while others suffer some unexpected financial hardship and can't afford to finish.

Very few clients will give the *real* reason for cancelling a lesson at short notice, or the remainder of the course, and the need for a suitable excuse is compelling.

The sudden death of a friend or relative is so common that I long ago started to call myself 'Doctor Death'. Mothers, fathers, brothers and sisters are never given as an excuse, but cousins, aunties, uncles and friends at work are definitely at some risk, and pass on at an alarming rate! In fact, at times they drop off at a rate that would rival the great plague! It seems that these people are expendable in terms of excuses.

I often worry that insurance firms may outlaw my training course if the remarkably high death rate of friends and relatives of my clients became common knowledge.

As the death rate has accelerated, I have developed a complex. Statistics show that one in five of my clients can expect such a death before completing my course. This curse on my course must almost rate with the curse of the Pharaohs. Imagine what *Ripley's Believe It or Not* or the *Guinness World Records* would do if they got hold of this information. My business would be ruined for all time.

Unfortunately, the problem is continuing, sometimes in plague proportions, and at other times only the odd soul departs to the hereafter at my expense. It does not appear to be seasonal. Losses can be expected at any time of the year.

As you can well imagine, this is a heavy cross for me to bear, and it is not a responsibility that I take lightly. However, I have been taught by a close friend to always endeavour to turn a negative situation into a plus, so I have decided to set up a company selling life insurance policies to friends and relatives of my clients.

After all, one in five clients who have a friend or relative who pass on is only 20%, and the other 80% will pay regular premiums.

Not a bad sideline for old Doctor Death?

# A LONELY LADY

THE TRAGEDY OF CRIME OF EVERY TYPE IS COMMONPLACE IN OUR SOCIETY—rape, armed hold-ups, break and enters, and murders are reported daily through news services. Although shocking to us, most of the time we are remote from these events, but our violent society seems even more chilling when such tragedy strikes a friend, relative or acquaintance.

One of my clients met her death in a bizarre manner some years ago, and her loss of life had a great impact on me because of the incidents leading up to her death.

The lady first contacted me with an enquiry for protection through my security company. She had suffered an attempt on her life from a former friend and was terrified of future attacks.

After speaking to her on the phone and making an appointment to meet with her I contacted the police to verify her story. That afternoon I arrived for the appointment, aware that her story was indeed true and her assailant had, in fact, been charged but released on bail pending a court hearing.

Before entering the house, I drove around the immediate neighbourhood checking the locale and the house itself to determine the best method of protection for the lady.

The home itself was a single-storey brick house with entrances available only through the front or rear doors. This type of dwelling was typical of the area with as many as ten houses in a row sharing common walls and each had a small backyard which backed onto a lane. I entered the front gate and knocked on the front door, deep in thought about the problem of protecting the lady on a twenty-four-hour-per-day basis as she had indicated she would need.

My train of thought was broken by the sliding of a chain and the opening of a lock and the door opened about three inches, the chain still in place. A lady peered anxiously around the door with an enquiring look upon her face.

I introduced myself and passed a business card through the door. The lady, now reassured, released the chain and opened the door, closing it quickly behind me and resetting the lock and chain. I waited as she completed the lock-up and then followed her through the house to a large lounge room.

The inside of the house was tastefully furnished with expensive furniture. Pastel colours dominated the walls and curtains giving a relaxed aura of quiet wealth.

The lady herself was a striking blonde of European extraction, possibly around the forty-year-old mark. She was dressed in a neat slack-suit and was adorned with a great deal of jewellery which to my untrained eye was obviously real and worth a great deal of money.

As I sat down on a single lounge chair the lady launched into her story leading up to the attempt on her life. As she related the incidents, she paced up and down, clasping and unclasping her hands in between nervous puffs on her cigarette.

After a lengthy discussion I decided that the best service I could offer would be a trained dog. At that time, I had several dogs trained for that type of work. The dogs were capable of living in a family environment and offered excellent protection at a fraction of the cost of an armed escort.

My client agreed to undertake a handling course with the dog and I rang my office immediately to have the dog delivered to her home. While waiting for the dog to arrive I explained the theory of the training and the handling and maintenance methods necessary to keep the dog in good health during its stay.

As I talked, the lady continued to pace up and down and I wasn't sure whether she was nervous about the dog or her past experiences. My doubts and her nervous attitude were relieved almost immediately with the arrival of her new canine bodyguard.

The dog was a four-year-old German Shepherd bitch named Tina who, like many properly trained dogs, belied her capabilities by her calm, friendly manner.

When Tina entered the room, my client was sitting on the lounge, engaged in a conversation on the phone, obviously distraught at some new piece of information she was being given. Tina, released from her lead, headed straight over to the woman, sniffed her shoe and, as if in instant approval, placed her paw on the lady's leg. She was given a hesitant pat and, taking this as an approval, Tina jumped onto the lounge and settled with her head on the lap of my amazed client.

Before the end of her telephone conversation Tina had stolen the heart of the lady who had already gained confidence from Tina's attitude. When the phone call ended Tina lifted her head and licked the lady's hand then settled her head down as if she had been reared from birth in the house.

My client had some doubts about Tina's attack training because of her gentleness but these doubts were quickly dispelled when I demonstrated the dog's ability in a training session with one of my mobile patrolmen who had been called in especially for the job.

The patrolman, protected by a training suit, crept into the backyard and Tina, under my control and witnessed by the doubting lady, confronted the prowler, cornered him and then, under direction, attacked and held until called off. She then placed herself near the prowler to one side of me in a perfect position to guard against either attack on us or escape attempts.

After the 'prowler' had been escorted off the premises, the dog returned inside with us and lay at the feet of the lady who had gained confidence from the demonstration and then the dog's ability to return to her normal state.

Over the next week the lady went through an intensive handling course and after a slow start became a fair handler and I felt she was competent to handle the dog in a real situation if she were attacked.

During the week the lady had expressed some fears regarding the ability of the person who had attacked her and his way with dogs. The man was originally from the country and had worked with dogs on properties for some time and was supposedly very confident with dogs of any size, shape or colour.

I explained that part of Tina's training was a developed wariness to any stranger to whom she hadn't been introduced, and that at no time, under any circumstances, was she to let this man touch the dog in a friendly manner or relaxed situation.

Three years later, after her death, I remembered *clearly* emphasising that point. I wish she had taken more notice at the time.

The dog was left in a live-in situation and for a month everything went fine, with the lady's tormentor phoning her at work and threatening or following her in his car occasionally, but no direct confrontations.

During this time, I kept in constant contact either by phone or by calling in to see how things were going—each time stressing that she should not relax her guard, and to keep the dog with her whenever possible, which was almost all the time.

Then I received a phone call one Saturday morning from the lady who was in an agitated state. The man had attempted to break into the house and had almost gained entry through a window at the rear. Tina had sprung from the lap of the lady who was watching television and had heard nothing. Tina had caught the man as he had started to climb through the window. The dog had bitten and held the man just under the armpit on the fleshy part of his back. The man's screams had stimulated the dog and the lady had some difficulty in calling the dog off and gaining some control.

As the dog released its grip the man tumbled backwards out of the window, clutching his side and bellowing with rage. The lady ran inside and called the police. The attacker had fled the scene long before they arrived but was later questioned over the attack and warned to keep away or the restraining order, that was already in existence, would be enforced to its full measure.

No further physical attacks occurred after this but the man kept up some constant form of harassment, either by phone or by his presence in some way, and always when the lady was on her own. The man seemed to have a sixth sense as to when someone else was present as we set up surveillance on many occasions without him showing.

After several months of this kind of harassment the lady finally gave in. Her physical health had suffered from the constant bombardment of abuse and her nerves were shot. At this point she phoned me and asked, regretfully, for me to pick up Tina as she was going away.

On arrival at her house, I was surprised to see that she had been waiting in an empty house for my arrival.

The deterioration in the lady's appearance over the previous months was evident with her face drawn and her shoulders stooped from the strain.

"Enough," she said. "I have had enough. The police, you and your men, the dog, I have had all the protection that is possible and still my life is under constant threat. I am leaving. I am going where no one will find me and no one will know me. I must have some peace of mind. I must live in a normal way, or my life is not worth living."

"What about the court case?" I replied. "They won't get a prosecution without your testimony."

"Yes, I know that," she said as she paced nervously around the room. "I have arranged for that. Here is a cheque to settle my account and I thank you for your service and your concern over my safety."

She paused again, this time to light a cigarette. "I have sold my business and made all other necessary arrangements. I am concerned only that I have to leave Tina." She then bent down and cuddled Tina briefly, and walked from the house and entered a waiting car which drove off immediately.

To be honest, I was somewhat relieved that my part in this job was over as I had felt a constant pressure since supplying the dog some months previously. I pondered then how my client must have felt as it was *her* life that was in constant danger, and it was she who had suffered the attacks and threats.

The lady left my life as quickly and dramatically as she had entered it, and I thought that I had heard the last of her. I was wrong. Almost three years later I received a phone call one Friday evening at midnight. It was the estranged lady, and again, her life was under threat.

During the time since I had last seen her, I had cancelled the service of renting guard dogs out on an extended basis, as I had done in her case. The reason for this was simple. The dogs, of which there were three, had been placed in similar situations in homes and lived as a family pet and protector. The problem was, in between jobs the dogs had to live in a kennel environment until the next job came up. It meant that the dogs were constantly bonding to a family or individual and then returning to the kennel, and I felt that it was unfair to the dogs.

I sold all the dogs to previous people who had utilised the service, and in that way the dogs lived a complete family life with no disruption.

That late-night phone call had broken my sleep and I was a little disorientated as I explained that I no longer could offer the service, but I did have a trained dog for sale.

I gave her the details of the dog and she agreed to buy him after first enquiring whether Tina was available. I asked for her address and she gave it to me, and then said she wanted the dog immediately as she was scared of being attacked again.

The thought of driving 40 miles across town to deliver a dog at midnight did not enthuse me at all and I tried to talk her into waiting till the morning. She pleaded with me to bring the dog over straight away and her fear sounded so real that I reluctantly agreed, and hung up to go and tell my disbelieving wife that I was going out to deliver a dog.

One of the reasons I did not want to deliver the dog at that time was that I had to enter the kennel area and disturb the other dogs, and chances were that they would not settle down again. Sure enough, when I went down for the dog, all hell broke loose and the barking was still audible when I drove out and headed for town.

An hour later I arrived at her new address and I was let into the house only after giving the pre-arranged signal at the front door. I can remember thinking that it all sounded like a badly written TV soap, what with late-night dog deliveries and secret knocks, etc.

The house I entered had little in common with the lady's previous house. In fact, it was rundown and in obvious need of repair. The paint on the walls and ceilings was discoloured through age and cheap curtains and threadbare carpet completed the setting. The simple furnishings were a complete reversal of the former luxury items which had been the order of the day at the lady's former address.

The lady herself had changed little in looks. Her striking good looks and figure were still intact but the jewellery which she had worn so well in the past was gone as were the expensively cut clothes.

It was when she spoke that I noticed the difference in her. She was remote, as if drunk or drugged, but there was no smell of liquor, and her movements were quick and sure. I looked at her eyes to see if her pupils were dilated. They weren't, but there was a deep hurt in her eyes, the type of look a dog gives when he is going to be put down and senses it.

I mentally braced myself to get on with the job at hand. The introduction with the dog went smoothly; the lady had lost none of her handling skills and we completed a handling lesson as best we could within the crowded lounge room.

Later, over a cup of tea, she brought me up to date on all the events since I had last seen her, and then I left after making an appointment for the next morning to team her and the dog together.

I staggered into bed over an hour later to be met with a wide-awake wife still disbelieving—even when I produced the cheque I had been given for the dog.

The reteam with the dog next morning went smoothly except that this time the lady was handling a male dog much bigger and stronger than Tina, and we had to work hard on her handling techniques before I was confident enough to leave her and the dog.

That night I received a call from the lady again in a state of agitation. The man had entered the backyard and had lay in wait until she opened the door. He had then tried to push his way in. He had gained entry after a brief struggle only to be attacked by the dog. The dog was controlled only after a great deal of effort on the part of the lady and her attacker fled the scene, shouting threats.

The threats in this case were aimed at me. It seemed he did not like being attacked while he was himself attacking, and the assault upon his person for the *second* time by one of my dogs was too much, hence the threats.

The lady was quite concerned. "He knows who you are and it won't take too long for him to find where you reside", she said.

I did not take these threats lightly as the man had shown a complete lack of respect for the law and he seemed driven by some maniacal desire of which I did not know the basis. I thanked the lady for her call and then took the precaution of sending my wife and son to her mother for the time being, as I could not leave the kennels unattended.

Over the next week I had several telephone conversations with the woman and on several occasions was puzzled by some of the statements that she made regarding the man, his activities and their relationship. As a result of these conversations, I formed the opinion that the woman was in some ways encouraging the attention of the man and then, depending on her mood, rejecting him coldly or sympathising with him. If this was indeed right it would explain the persistent inconsistency of the man's behaviour.

Some two weeks after the attack I received another late-night phone call from the lady requesting that I deliver her another dog. This call took me completely by surprise as did her answer to the reason for the request. It seemed that the man had turned up that night and after an extended conversation on the front veranda she had invited him into the house to talk things over, and an hour later allowed him to handle the dog.

The dog had been lying beside her, under control, during the talk and in the relaxed situation, and with the lady agreeing, the man had picked up the dog's leash and walked the dog around the house. After this, he sat and patted the dog for half an hour before leaving.

After he had left the lady worried whether she had done the right thing or not.

Her worries were soon confirmed by a phone call from the man. He told her that now the dog was his friend, and the next time he came in, he would kill her. He then hung up and the woman phoned me.

"Why would you let him in? And worse still, why would you let him handle the dog?" I exclaimed with exasperation. "That dog was your best form of defence and what you have done goes against *everything* I have taught you during the time you have been handling the dog. I can't understand how you could do such a stupid thing," I concluded.

The lady was in tears now. It was the first time since I had been dealing with her that she had actually broken down.

"Well, what would you have done?" she said tearfully. "He takes no notice of the police and I am under constant threat the whole time. I thought maybe if I could talk to him without the threat of violence that he may leave me alone."

I couldn't understand the logic in what she said, but then again, my life hadn't been under the threat of death continuously for an extended period of time like hers had been, and I didn't know all the details of their previous relationship.

Dogs of the type that she had been sold were not readily available. They were then—and are now—a rare commodity. It would be a good business to have these types of dogs for sale on a regular basis, but it is not possible to mass produce dogs trained to this standard. People under pressure often make bad decisions, and I tried hard to understand her actions, but now I had no way to help her. She had put herself in a much more vulnerable position.

I continued the conversation for a few more minutes and then the lady hung up abruptly while I was in mid-sentence. I rang back immediately but there was no answer and subsequent calls over the next two days were the same.

The climax of this tragedy was realised a day or so later. I had picked up the daily newspaper after tea and settled in front of the TV with a cup of tea.

The headlines carried the story of a lady who had been shot dead by a former boyfriend who then turned the gun on himself.

At first it didn't register with me but as I read the article, I realised that the lady was in fact my former client. Names released by the police later that night confirmed this.

I rang through to the police to find out the whereabouts of the dog, but I was told that there was no dog on the premises when they arrived.

I never did find out what happened to the dog. Hopefully some family member is caring for him.

# DOULTON THE WONDER DOG

MY CLIENTS ASK MANY QUESTIONS during training, but by far the most common question is, "What breed of dog do you have yourself?"

I have owned many types of dogs over the years, pure, cross and mixed breeds, but I have a strong bias towards German Shepherds, and I prefer a gentle bitch.

Sometime ago, Gypsy, my faithful companion of many years, had developed mammary cancer, and I had given her the freedom she deserved when the pain was obvious. She was twelve years old, and I could not give thought to owning a puppy after 'Gyppo' was gone, and declared that I would *never* have another dog.

Still, the clients ask me about my dog, and of course, I still had Doulton, another German Shepherd. Was he well trained, house-trained, destructive?—and a million other questions about his behaviour were all asked repeatedly.

To be honest, Doulton was a Wonder Dog, who never blemished his copy book at any time—even as a youngster. He had never soiled a rug, chewed a shoe, bitten a postman, or barked or howled. Doulton is, indeed, the perfect dog, as would be expected.

What I never told the clients, of course, was that he was a Royal Doulton—a porcelain China dog, who sits upon my TV and gazes regally across the room.

Now, I know he is an inanimate object, but I am still attached to old Doulton the Wonder Dog.

🐾🐾

# ANDREW DARLING

THE LAST LESSON OF THE DAY. Winter had arrived with a vengeance. The sunlight was already fading and the shadows were creeping steadily across the road as I pulled up outside the address of a new client. I knocked on the door, and studied tile grounds, as I waited for an answer.

The house was a modest, semi-detached dwelling with neat gardens and an ornamental slate mailbox that looked like a form of modern art gone wrong. The door swung open and a young boy of about fourteen eyed me with annoyance. "Yeah, what do you want?" he asked as he looked me over. Before I could answer, a high-pitched voice echoed down the hallway. "That will be Mr Fraser, the dog trainer, Andrew, darling, please bring him through."

Andrew looked me over again, holding my gaze with an insolent glare. He was a skinny boy, tall for his age, and well dressed with his hair neatly combed. He scanned me up and down again, with a look that made my skin crawl. He stepped aside grudgingly and I walked down the narrow hallway to the living room area, where his mother was waving, clutching a small terrier to her chest.

She was stroking the dog on the head as I introduced myself, when she guided me to a chair at the table, and switched the overhead light on. The woman stood, patting the dog and beaming. "Mummy's little baby is not going to school—King is," she cried to the dog in a soft, sing-song voice. I sat down and arranged my paperwork in front of me as the woman continued talking baby talk to her dog. The dog nestled into her chest, licking at her hand contentedly.

She then took her kettle down and lit the stove, set out the cups, milk, sugar and biscuits, all with one hand as she held on to the dog. The boy was standing near the back door, now smiling at me, as she opened the door.

As the door opened, a huge male German Shepherd bounded through the door and stood inspecting me with his tail curved up over his back in an arrogant stance. I had no doubt the dog was anti-social and he made straight for me, bobbing under the table and sniffing my legs.

I sat still with my hands on the table as he continued sniffing, working his way up my legs and nosing into my crotch, while emitting a soft, but definite growl. I sat, almost paralysed, the sweat beads popping out on my forehead, and the hair standing up on the nape of my neck. The dog continued his intimate inspection as I sat, statue-like, not game to move a muscle.

I knew any form of withdrawal would spark an avalanche of aggression, and at this point, the dog definitely held all the aces. I slowly turned my head towards the woman, hoping for some form of relief. She had her back to me, busily making the tea. She was talking to me, but I lost the conversation's context when the dog started his intimate body search.

Andrew 'darling' remained at the door, watching for any reaction with interest; he smiled and stood slightly bemused, with a disappointed look on his face. With no hope of immediate help from the family, I glanced down at my lap, where the dog had his head firmly wedged, still growling. I looked him directly in the eye, for all of half a second, before I closed my eyes and took a deep breath, as I struggled to remain calmly seated.

The dog had light-coloured eyes, filled with malice. I knew that he was experienced at this type of confrontation, and I could also tell that he was a champion of such encounters.

The nerve in my leg twitched, and my knee jerked involuntarily, which prompted a deep-throated growl from the dog, and a wicked smile from Andrew 'darling', who was obviously enjoying this new development very much.

The woman turned slightly at the sound of the growl, and my hopes for a merciful rescue jumped, but she turned back to the sink, and continued her one-sided conversation, dashing my hopes immediately. I don't claim to be a devout Christian, although I try as best as I can to live within the values, and I couldn't remember the last time I prayed. But I had lost none of the basics and I quickly and silently laid out my case. Like all people in a corner who appeal to the higher being, I wished I had been a little more consistent in my communication with God, and of course vowed I would be in the future, if my appeal was given favourable consideration.

The sweat was now pouring down my forehead, little rivulets flowing into my eyes, their salty contents stinging my eyes. The dog had not moved, and I could feel his eyes boring up into my face; he shifted his weight, and leaned heavily against my leg.

The lady turned, and moved slowly to the table, carrying the teapot, not noticing my plight. She placed the teapot on the table and pulled a chair out, before she noticed the dog under the table. "Oh, you have met King, have you? That's most unusual, he

usually attacks people, but it seems he has taken a shine to you—isn't he cute, resting his head like that?"

"Yes, he is a nice dog," I said in what I hoped was a controlled voice. "Perhaps we could put him outside while we talk about our pupil?"

"Yes, that's a good idea. Andrew, darling, just put King outside while we talk now, that's a good boy."

Andrew slouched against the doorway, unimpressed by his mother's request. "Gee, Mum, King likes to stay in, and he seems to really like the trainer." His mum nodded in agreement as she poured the tea.

"All right, Andrew, darling, we will let him stay in for a while, he seems to like Mr Fraser." She turned to me and lowered her voice confidentially, "Andrew's such a good boy, not cheeky or nasty or bold like a lot of boys are nowadays. I am so lucky he is the way he is, aren't I?"

I sat immobile while King investigated new areas around my navel, and I then looked up to Andrew 'darling', who changed his position slightly, and gave me a smiling look, obviously delighted by my situation.

An answer was obviously expected from the lady's question, and I nodded my head in agreement before starting on the training information. As it turned out, the training of the dog proved to be no real problem. Like many dogs who are territorial, he responded to pack leadership, and was very receptive to training.

Andrew 'darling' proved to be a good handler, but his attitude remained the same, and I would have dearly liked the opportunity to give him some compulsive training. That incident happened more than a decade ago, and I forgot about it until recently.

I had arrived at the house of a new client, a married couple in an area on the outskirts of Sydney.

The young couple owned a small dog who had no real problems and just needed some basic obedience training. I gained the profile information over a cup of tea and biscuits, and I thought that this young couple had their act together and were obviously handling life very well indeed.

The husband owned his own small business, and we shared a common interest in restoring old cars. The lesson went well, and I established a strong liking for this easy-going youngster.

As I was leaving, I asked him where he had found my name, as I like to keep track of what sources my clients usually come from.

He smiled and slouched against the wall, and the stance seemed vaguely familiar. "You might not remember, but you trained my mother's dog a long time ago."

The stance was what triggered my memory—twelve years on, he still slouched against the wall in the same way, but an open, friendly smile had replaced the insolent, smug look.

There stood Andrew 'darling', the finished product, and a nicer young man would be hard to find.

# AUSSIE REVENGE

MY ARRIVAL HOME AT THE END OF A DAY TRAINING DOGS is nowhere near the end of my working day. There are usually at least a half a dozen phone calls regarding training enquiries to be made, and then, of course, the phone seems to ring incessantly.

I arrived home late one winter's night and was just settling down to a cup of tea and some television when the phone rang. The enquiry was from an English chap who had a large cross-breed dog who was biting him. The problem was straightforward, and after discussing some details on training and behaviour modification, the man made an appointment for early the next week.

For some reason when I took the man's particulars I never asked for his surname. I duly arrived at the house and quickly reviewed the details of the call to refresh my memory and then walked up the driveway of a neat brick home.

My knock was answered immediately by the man's wife who greeted me and then ushered me through to the lounge room. We sat and talked for a few minutes while her husband completed a phone call in the next room before he joined us.

As he walked through the door with his hand outstretched in greeting, I recognised him—he was a former English Test cricket batsman! We sat down and started on the profile information I required before the start of training.

He told me again of the biting problem and said that he was relieved that I could solve the problem. Well, I wasn't about to let him off the hook that easy; this was not just another client—this was a Pommie batsman who had whacked our best bowlers all around playing fields throughout Australia and England. I'd seen him on many occasions in full flight, frustrating our bowlers and punishing them and the fieldsmen who chased speeding balls all around the oval.

I sat deep in thought for a moment and then decided to have a bit of fun at his expense. "The problem may not be as easy to solve as I first thought," I said seriously. I watched his expression carefully as I made my statement; he was hooked, taken in by my serious expression. He cocked his head, obviously confused after my statements in our telephone conversation.

"I see. I had thought from our earlier conversation that it was to be a simple matter of gaining control through obedience and establishing myself as pack leader!" He leant back and crossed his arms, questioning my statement.

"Well, you see, it's a matter of ethics; after all, the dog is an Aussie, and you being an ex-Pommie cricketer it could almost be regarded as an act of disloyalty to the flag, so to speak, if I were to stop the dog biting you. Just put yourself in my position," I continued. "What would the papers say if they got hold of this—cricket fans all around the country would be after my blood!" His face broke into a broad grin as he realised that I had conned him.

"Yes, I can see that you would have a problem, but I tell you what, I won't tell anyone if you don't."

Over a period of the next six weeks the dog was trained in weekly lessons. The man showed some ability with the lead and quickly learned to control the difficult and aggressive dog. We spent many hours walking through his suburb, discussing cricket and sport in general, and a few hours more over tea and biscuits at his house.

At the end of our lessons, I had established a firm friendship with him, and admired him for the way he had stuck to a difficult and somewhat painful task in completing the training. At the end of the last lesson, we stood on his front lawn with the dog lying obediently at his feet.

"Just one more thing regarding the dog," I said smugly. "I've done a bit of secret training at the other end of the park, you remember when I walked away without you?"

He nodded his head in agreement, his forehead creased in puzzlement.

"Well," I continued. "I don't want you to think that you can get away scot-free just because we've become friends, so I have trained the dog to attack you any time you say 'Aussie bastards', so be careful he's outside when you're watching the Test matches on the television!"

# COOKIES

My views on the use of food reward in training have already been described, but in one session, food reward produced a comical result.

The client was a middle-aged South American lady, who was as wide as she was tall. The woman had a habit of talking with her hands, and every sentence was emphasised with a high-pitched voice and wild hand gestures. Her high-pitched giggle produced a massive shaking of her body; this was coupled with both of her hands waving around, and was a sight to behold.

She also had a habit of holding on to whoever was near to her when she broke into these spasms of laughter. The first time she grabbed hold of me, I felt like I was plugged into a pneumatic drill! I was involuntarily bounced up and down, in time with her.

The lady owned a huge male Rottweiler who was progressing well in training but periodically appeared to lose concentration and jumped excitedly all over the woman. When this happened, the woman lost composure, and her battle to regain control over the dog was peppered by strings of abuse in her language, which echoed around the park.

The first time the lady broke into this tirade of abuse to her dog, we had been walking down the street with the woman handling the dog at the heel position. I was busy explaining a point when the woman exploded. She screamed and kicked out at the dog, and she shook a pointed finger at her canine companion.

Rottweilers' tails are cropped, and though he lacked a tail, he wagged from the hips down and seemed quite happy with himself despite the woman's abuse.

Some time later, when the woman had become a little more subdued, I was told in curt tones what the dog had done to promote her anger.

While walking beside her, he had cocked his leg and urinated on her foot, half-filling her shoe. This had been done while he had been on the move, and I never even noticed, as he didn't falter in any way.

After the incident, the woman was quite obviously angry at the dog, and we walked on in silence, apart from the squelching noise emanating from her sodden left shoe.

At the park, the dog continued to jump on the lady now and then, and I decided to observe closely what stimulated the dog to do this frantic activity. I was standing close to the lady, and she had handled the dog through an extended stay, recall and a perfect sit in front of her. She said something to the dog in Spanish, and the dog went berserk, jumping all over her and licking her as she continued repeating the Spanish phrase she had used when the dog started the activity.

After some calm had been restored and the lady had regained her breath, I asked her what she had said to the dog to trigger his reactions. She told me the meaning of the Spanish term she had used; it meant 'two cookies'. Throughout the lesson, she had kept score, adding cookies when the dog was good and subtracting them when the dog went out of control.

The dog was offered a cookie when he did something to please her, and the offer was removed when the dog reacted—but the retracting of the offer still retained the keyword, which stimulated the dog to further excitement. I explained this to the woman, along with a demonstration to prove my point, but my point was lost, as we never achieved a lesson without offering the two cookies and the excited reaction.

To my knowledge, the woman is still walking the streets, her left shoe sodden, and her dog waiting in anticipation for his cookies.

# BUSTED

IT WAS MY SECOND TRAINING JOB OF THE DAY, and the weather had changed ominously over the last ten minutes.

Black, angry clouds rolled across the sky and gusty winds were building in intensity as I pulled up outside the home of a new client. The home was in the inner-city area, an older suburb where most of the homes were double brick, built on large blocks.

I collected my paperwork and leads and made my way to the front door, greeted by a friendly, middle-aged lady who welcomed me into the house and showed me into the lounge room, featuring tasteful antique furniture.

I had gathered most of the information regarding the dog's habits on our initial phone conversation. This would be a simple obedience training program, which

would be completed over the customary six weeks. We had a brief discussion about her responsibilities in practising in between sessions, and I was introduced to the dog, a quiet Cavalier King Charles Spaniel, one of my favourite breeds.

As we left the house, I noticed that the storm that had threatened prior to my entering had passed over. Although it was still overcast, there did not appear to be a threat of rain.

The lesson went well. Both the dog and the handler were receptive to my training methods, and the woman was very consistent in her commands and handling methods.

The next two lessons were uneventful, and the dog progressed each week, as the lady was obviously practising in between sessions. As we were walking with the dog in our lessons, the lady conversed openly regarding her business—supplying office supplies directly to businesses and schools. At the time, I thought she was your average, middle-aged businesswoman, leading a quiet, normal life.

That all changed in the next lesson, when as we were leaving the house, two men stopped us and showed identification indicating they were state police detectives and were there to arrest the woman for large-scale drug supply.

The lady was quickly moved inside to another room, and I was still standing outside the front door, dumbstruck by the events that had just taken place.

The policeman with me then asked for my identification, my relationship with the woman, and my reason for being there that day.

I explained my position and gave him the number of a detective mate of mine to verify my occupation and why I would be at the house.

The detective asked for my phone number and told me I could leave and that he would be in touch if he needed to talk again.

Before I left for my next job, I reflected on the events of the last half hour and concluded that there must have been a mistake in the information they had collected on the woman.

During my time with her, she displayed no obvious criminal tendencies—on the contrary, I would have described her as a well-adjusted, 'model' citizen.

I drove on, contemplating that I would get a phone call from a somewhat embarrassed client in the next day or so.

The phone call never came—the woman had been distributing cocaine and was found guilty and sentenced to a long term in prison.

The lady had paid for the training in advance and still had three lessons in credit, which she is welcome to use any time.

# FUNNIES AND FAUX PAS

As you have read, my training method, giving private lessons at people's houses, means that I encounter a broad cross-section of the community.

In one day, clients can range from the average family, to leading Kings' Counsels and barristers, and my next job may well be with someone on the fringe of the underworld.

Localities also change, and I may travel from a struggling lower-income area to an exclusive and more prosperous suburb.

In short, I *never* know who is on the other end of the line when I receive a phone call. For these reasons I have had some amusing incidents from this potpourri of a community. I will recount some here.

I recently received a call about training a dog for protection work. The owner was a man who earned his living in a way that society would have frowned upon. He was a likeable knock-about type who kept a low profile on his business activities and personal life.

Like many hard cases, he had a natural affinity with his dog and spent many hours training and exercising it. The dog was flighty around people, especially crowds, so before any protection training began, we had to spend some time walking the dog through crowded areas to make sure there would be no unpredictable reactions.

Over a couple of weeks, the dog settled down, and I was pleased with its progress. We had been walking through congested shopping centres, and the dog learned to ignore screaming children, joggers, pedestrians and harried housewives toting the week's shopping. After a few weeks of this, the dog accepted everybody, and any situation, that arose.

One day, while walking the dog through a busy city street, we stopped at an intersection and waited for the lights to change. The dog sat obediently beside me and waited patiently for the next command. I was somewhat surprised when he growled at the person beside us. The dog was not at all happy about the man and I corrected him, with no result.

I looked at the man, who seemed vaguely familiar, and I searched my memory, trying to put a name to the face. The man stood, quietly relaxed and not intimidated by the dog's continued growling. It was then that I put a name to the face—he was a well-known criminal and suspected hitman who had received considerable adverse publicity over the years.

As it turned out the owner of the dog and the man were on speaking terms, and they exchanged greetings. As the lights changed and the man walked off, he showed that whatever he was in private life, he did not lack a sense of humour. He smiled at my client and said, "You'd better keep that dog, mate, he's a bloody good judge of character!"

Phone calls are usually my first introduction to clients, and I committed a memorable faux pas in one of these phone conversations.

The man enquiring had a dog who had harassed a tradesman, and although the dog had not bitten in this instance, he was worried that the dog might in the future. We discussed the dog's background and some training methods during the conversation.

As usual in this type of conversation relating to biting dogs, I went on and mentioned owner responsibility and gave some details of the local requirements and the law, the NSW Dog Act.

The man listened patiently throughout without making any comments. He agreed to a consultation to discuss the dog's problems further, and it was when I took his name and address that I realized my faux pas.

The man was an eminent Queen's Counsel who patiently listened to me rambling on about legal matters without comment. He was certainly much more gracious to me than many of the witnesses he had cross-examined. Although he had the reputation of a tough man, he let me off the hook without embarrassment.

The ladies of the night have proved to be rather offbeat in their attitude to dog training, which has caused some amusing incidents. One such lady had an oversized Doberman with an ego to match its size.

The dog strained continuously at the lead, surging forward, utilising its weight to its own advantage. It weighed about 40 kg and was very difficult to control.

Several times while we were walking the dog down the street, the lady had climbed a front fence and helped herself to whatever flowers took her fancy. I found this practice to be embarrassing and asked her not to do it while she was with me—a request to which she reluctantly agreed.

The training proved difficult but finally, after much effort on both our parts, the dog was walking perfectly at the heel position. At the end of the lesson, I stressed the need for consistency and left feeling well satisfied.

At the start of the next lesson, I was surprised and somewhat annoyed to find that the dog surged forward, pulling on the lead. I realised that the consistency I had stressed had not been adhered to, and questioned the young lady as to why.

Over the years of training dogs, I have had some excellent excuses offered as to why training routines had been changed, left in abeyance or just not bothered with, but this one was a real gem. Without any hesitation or embarrassment, the girl stated that it had only happened once. She said, "Well, I was walking down the street, and I stole so many flowers that I couldn't carry them and control the dog simultaneously!"

One of my jobs took me to a five-acre property on the outskirts of Sydney. The clients were two ladies in their thirties who lived in a neat fibro house at the rear of the property. The lessons were all early morning appointments, at 7:30 a.m., which enabled them to get to work on time.

At the first two lessons I was surprised, as the two women continually drank beer throughout the lesson. Tin after tin was downed, without any effect, and the time of the morning seemed like normal drinking time. It appeared to me that beer was their staple breakfast diet.

On the third lesson I arrived, and no one was in sight. My first knock at the door went unanswered, so my knocking became progressively louder until finally, an irate voice, coupled with some rather coarse language, made me cease.

The door swung open and a decidedly dishevelled, red-eyed and irate client looked at me with undisguised annoyance. Trying to make light of the situation I made some light-hearted remarks about her appearance and a hard night.

This was without a doubt the wrong approach. People who know me can attest to the fact that I sometimes misread situations and make inappropriate remarks.

In this case this was definitely true, and a vitriolic blast reinforced the withering glance I received for my comment. At this point her friend erupted through the door, fixed me with a menacing glare and added her thoughts on the subject:

"Listen, mate, if I were you, when I come knocking on a door, I would do just that—*knock*—don't try and kick the bloody thing off its hinges, understand?"

Well, of course I understood; I also understood that I didn't really need this type of aggro this early in the morning and was about to say so when their anger died and they became their usual friendly selves. "How about a cup of tea, mate?" the first lady said as the second stumbled back through the door to make herself presentable.

After a cup of tea and a quick spruce-up they were ready for the lesson. The transformation from their first appearance to the start of the lesson was nothing short of incredible. A quick wash, a change of clothes, a cup of tea (with a beer chaser) and they looked human again. A Hollywood make-up artist would have been proud of the job.

The lesson went without incident, and the two, who were both sales representatives, chatted lightly about the promotionl event that they attended the night before.

As I left after the completion of the lesson, I was laughingly told not to kick the door in on my next visit.

My next appointment at that property was preceded by two days of heavy rain. As I rode out to the property the next morning, I had to negotiate my motorcycle through a series of potholes in the road that led to the property.

The house was set well back on the property, and I eased the bike down into first gear and negotiated the greasy road, avoiding puddles which were of uncertain depth. The mud splashed up over my shoes and the undercarriage of the bike—it would dry to a thick coating if I didn't wash it off before it set.

I surveyed the grounds ahead and decided to pull up on the grass strip which ran beside the house and between the road. The strip of grass was about thirty feet wide and looked to be fairly firm and was sloped, so I expected a fair bit of run-off of the rain and firm underground. The grass looked firm but as the front wheel hit it, the top layer separated, revealing a layer of slippery clay underneath.

I could feel the bike slipping, and momentarily fought for control—a front wheel slip on a motorcycle is virtually uncontrollable, even at this low speed. Accelerating out is unthinkable, as the power given to the back wheel without control of the front would be a recipe for instant disaster. The application of brakes either front or back would have been virtually useless.

The momentum of the bike and the front wheel slipping had caught me in a hopeless situation so I hit the kill switch on the motor and lay the bike down. As it went down, I prayed that the soft grass held no hidden stones that would ruin the paintwork on my beloved machine.

I came off the cycle without effort; there was little chance of any physical injury but my pride was already suffering. Falling off a cycle is not good for a rider's self-esteem at any time, but to fall off at this low speed while riding down a deserted road was not exactly ego-building.

I hit the ground on hands and knees, a perfect four-point landing, leaving my now silent cycle behind me wedged firmly in the mud. As I hit the ground, my body weight increased my forward momentum and my speed accelerated at an alarming rate. I skidded towards the home, desperately trying to control my direction and slow my progress. This was to no avail and the side of the house loomed large in front of me, as the mud sprayed up all over me. I was feeling wet, cold and miserable.

The wall was nearer now, a collision was imminent and the manufacturer's claim about tile durability of my helmet was about to be tested. I hit the wall with a resounding crash and rolled onto my side in the mud with water slowly seeping through my clothes. Any thought of being able to hide the spill from my clients had disappeared with the sound of the impact.

I lay there momentarily and mentally completed a check-list which told me I had suffered no major physical damage, and slowly crawled to my knees.

As I looked up, my two clients were standing at the end of the house some ten feet away; they stood unsmiling, taking in the scene, the ever-present cans of beer in their hands.

Neither made a comment as I struggled to my feet—trying to recover some dignity from the situation.

"I slipped … the bike hit the clay … I had no control. …" I stammered. They looked me over quietly as I stood before them dripping mud, a sorrowful and sorry sight. The silence stretched interminably. Finally, one commented to the other, "It's your fault, Mary, you told him not to knock the door down, and you know how he likes to make a grand entrance."

Mary nodded her head in agreement and replied, "Yeah, you gotta hand it to the boy, he's got a lot of class when he comes visiting, he's got some style." With that she turned towards me. "Bathroom's in there, mate, towel's on the ring. I'll put the kettle on, make a mess on my bloody carpet and I'll kill yuh!"

On yet another occasion I misread a situation which got me right offside with a client. I had worked for the first four lessons with the woman of the family and the husband was going to participate in the fifth lesson.

The family lived in a huge old house in a fashionable suburb; they had in fact moved into this house in between lessons, so this was my first visit to the new house. The husband showed me around the place, bursting with pride and enthusiasm, as he pointed out the many advantages of the type of building and its superior craftsmanship.

This type of house held no appeal for me personally; the high ceilings and draughty rooms were far removed from the modern conveniences with which I surround myself at every opportunity.

The house was set on superb lawns with manicured gardens but there needed to be more atmosphere, and although I could appreciate the superior architecture, the house lacked practicality, in my point of view.

The tour seemed to go on forever as the man expounded the advantages of every room. As we reached the last room, he asked me my opinion, which I gave him without hesitation, and which I thought would please him.

"Yeah, mate," I said. "I can understand how you feel, to take a house like this and restore it will give you a great deal of satisfaction. I can identify with what you want to do, I restore vintage motorcycles for a hobby. The work's hard but the product's worth all the sweat. You have taken on a big project, but it will be worth it when it's finished!"

This was met with a stony silence which continued throughout the lesson. I realised that I had said something to upset the man, and could only think that my comparison to restoring old motorcycles to him restoring his lovely old home must have upset him.

The next lesson was with the wife only, and as we sat down to a cup of tea after the lesson the woman explained her husband's reaction. She told me between giggles that an architect had been employed and supervised a restoration project at a cost of over $150,000—this had been completed *before* my inspection and before my opinion had been asked for.

"Oh well, I'm only a dog trainer—what do I know about Federation architecture!"

# MAN AND DOG

A PERSISTENT LOUD KNOCKING ON THE FRONT DOOR at 1:15 a.m. is an ominous sound. I had been settled in a deep sleep for over an hour and was reluctant to accept such an intrusion.

I struggled to my feet, and slowly shuffled to the door, thinking that maybe some motorist had run out of petrol and needed a phone.

I switched on the front light, and shook my head, trying to clear the cobwebs. Two policemen armed with torches confronted me, and I knew from their manner that they were the bearers of bad news.

A young man who lived in a small dwelling at the rear of our five-acre property had been involved in a motor accident, and had been killed.

At eighteen, Bill was a bright youngster, with a carefree attitude to life that is envied by many of us adults with families, mortgages and only memories of that long-ago teenage period. His life revolved around his dog, his girlfriend and his work as a dog trainer, for which he had a natural ability.

I stood there, trying to come to terms with the fact that Bill was dead, rubbing my eyes, and thinking that maybe it was just a bad dream. The police needed information about Bill's family, which I supplied, and they left to inform his parents.

Three days later, the shock of the tragedy became a reality that was culminating in the youngster's funeral.

I made the trip to the cemetery by myself, as my wife was pregnant and unable to attend.

I stood awkwardly outside the chapel, unable to communicate with Bill's family, who were surrounded by grieving friends and relatives. Finally, I moved inside, and found my way to a vacant pew near the front of the chapel.

The mourners filed in through the doorway, heads bowed and silent as they filled the pews and stood against the walls. Many of the mourners were teenagers who had come to pay their last respects to the young friend who had been tragically killed.

I sat silently and stared at the coffin and thought about the young man who had been taken so suddenly,

My first recollections of Bill were a little clouded. He arrived in our group as the boyfriend of my mate's daughter and showed a natural ability with dogs that few people are lucky enough to be born with.

My friend, the girl's father, a professional trainer, was quick to spot Bill's potential. He employed him at the kennels and became his mentor, spending countless hours teaching him his craft.

Bill's enthusiasm for training was overridden by a youthful naivety and the ability to question the mechanics of every task that was carried out in the kennels. This questioning attitude had often become the focal point of the day's work as Bill's standard, "But why does it have to be done that way?" was repeated at regular intervals throughout the day.

The occupation of a dog trainer working in training kennels is an unusual one, and a result is achieved by team effort of the staff. Certain monotonous jobs must be carried out each day, so that the appearance of the property and the hygiene of the dog are maintained.

Although the work is consistent, there are many lighter moments. The level of camaraderie at this kennel was high, with practical jokes and verbal sledging of the staff rampant. Everybody was the butt of various situations at different times, and Bill had his fair share, along with the rest of us.

One of the training specialties of the kennels was training dogs to work with the patrolmen in the security fields. These dogs are attack-trained for this work, and the dogs selected are strong physically and usually aggressive by nature.

On one morning, Bill was still cleaning the kennels, while the other staff were having their morning tea break, and he fell over and trod on a dog's tail, who promptly attacked him. He was bitten badly several times on the buttocks and the leg, and on the arm and the back for good measure. To his credit, he managed to secure the dog in the kennel and came up to the office unaided.

He walked in the doorway with an expression of shock and pain on his face and announced that he had been bitten. Fresh puncture marks covered his body, and he was a sad and sorry sight. He had been warned that this was a possibility, but with supreme youthful confidence, he had stated, "No way, I won't get bitten, no way." Subsequent suggestions to be careful around the dog met with a contemptuous glance from young Bill.

Well, his day had arrived, and he had been bitten, and he was not happy about it. Most of the other trainers had been bitten during training, and often the shock of being attacked is as bad as the pain. The one important thing is not to lose confidence.

Riders who fall off a horse are advised to get straight back on it, if possible, and bitten dog trainers should gain control of their problem dog if attacked. Bill's wounds were attended to as he sat silently, studying the lacerations, which had been saturated with Dettol. One of the staff took him to the hospital for a tetanus injection and he returned full of stitches, and in a subdued mood.

Dog bites always seem to hurt more an hour or so after the attack. An hour had passed since he was attacked, sutured and needled, as we sat quietly with him, questioning what had happened.

He was advised that he should now handle the dog to regain his confidence. He agreed without hesitation and for a fleeting moment, regained his former cocky attitude, picked up a lead and strolled confidently towards the kennels without a backward glance. We stood and watched him as he neared the kennel gates, and without so much as a break in his stride, he entered the kennel area.

"That boy's got guts, even if he is a bit raw," one of the kennel hands stated as Bill disappeared behind the kennel wall. We stood talking, all understanding that this was a difficult test for an inexperienced trainer, who had just suffered a severe attack. The handling of the dog was something that had to be done on his own, and in reality, his future as a trainer was on the line because if his nerve broke, he may never again confidently master an aggressive dog.

The seconds dragged past slowly as we watched down the kennel area, all silently hoping that Bill would pass his trial.

The kennel wall was shoulder-high and was built as an effective screen to keep the dogs from reacting noisily to strangers in the office area. Although we could see a percentage of the area, we could not see the area completely, and it seemed an eternity before we saw any movement. The silence in the office hung heavy, as we had all suffered the same trial at various times after being attacked, with varying degrees of severity. Now a young colleague was on trial, and we stood, willing him to come to grips with the situation and control the dog.

Then Bill's head came into view, flashing across the top of the wall at great speed, running hard. "He's chasing the dog!" came a cry. "See how determined he is!" added somebody. "Gee, he can move!" added another. The mood in the office was elated that Bill had apparently passed his test, and bluffed the dog.

He disappeared for a few seconds, and then reappeared, still running determinedly; his speed had not decreased by a fraction, as he became visible for a third time, as he lapped the exercise compound.

The realisation slowly set in, and we all reacted by running from the office; Bill seemed to be in trouble.

We ran towards the compound, all the staff ready to give assistance if needed. We reached the wall almost as a single unit, as Bill completed yet another lap with an irate dog close at his heels. As he ran, he was pushing on kennel doors, hoping to find an empty one so that he could gain sanctuary from the aggressive canine, who seemed intent upon inflicting even more injuries upon the luckless youngster.

His breath was ragged, and he seemed about to lose ground, when with a superhuman effort, he scrambled over the brick fence, and tumbled to the grass below our feet.

He lay there for a moment, then stood up, dusted himself off, looked at us defiantly, and then strolled up to the office without saying a word.

Bill had subsequently handled that dog, and many more equally aggressive animals. He had faced his test, and earned the respect of his fellow trainers, through his determination and courage. He bore the scars of his ordeal like medals, and was quite ready to disrobe and show anybody who was the slightest bit interested.

At a later stage, he had been teamed with his own dog, to whom he was devoted, and who rarely left his side.

The muted organ music shattered my reminiscing thoughts as the minister moved into position and the service commenced.

The service was unique as an unusual request had been made to, and granted by, the compassionate minister.

As a sign of respect, Bill's dog was present at the funeral ceremony, accompanied by Bill's mentor, who arrived dressed in full security uniform.

The dog and handler were in the front row, and the dog lay silently, his head resting on his paws, almost in a praying position.

The sun shone through the stained-glass window, and encased both coffin and dog in a soft yellow blaze, highlighting them in the dimness of the chapel, man and dog together until the end.

# MANFRED'S DOG

I WAS WORKING IN MY TRAINING KENNELS one morning when I had a phone call from a teammate from the football club I was playing with; he asked if I could supply him with a dog that would protect his wife while he was away overseas.

Manfred had been selected in the 1974 World Cup Squad, which was due to travel to Germany for the World Cup Finals series. Depending on the results they gained in the opening group stage, the team would be away for two to three weeks, and he was worried about his wife being home with two young children.

As he recited exactly what was required of the dog, I listened in amused silence as he rattled off his list of must-haves regarding the dog's behaviour, house training, demeanour, protective qualities, etc. The list seemed never-ending, but he finally stopped and hesitated before commenting that it would be good if the dog also responded to commands given in German!

I shook my head in amazement at his naivety in what he had requested; the chances of finding a suitable dog with all the qualities he required were *nil*, especially as he was leaving on his trip one week later.

I told him I would do my best, but also mentioned that the chances were slim; he laughed and commented that I would find a suitable dog.

The task and the timeline given seemed impossible, but a few days later I received a call from a vet friend of mine who had a client who was moving overseas and had an adult

German Shepherd they wanted to place in a home.

He gave me the woman's number, and I phoned and arranged to view the dog that afternoon. I was hoping the dog would have at least *some* of the qualities that Manfred required, including some protective qualities, a stable temperament, and fit into the family situation.

On arrival at the house, I was greeted by a middle-aged woman and the dog, who eyed me cautiously before approaching and accepting a pat.

The woman explained the situation and gave me a detailed rundown on the dog's feeding, medications and behaviour traits. During this time the dog sat calmly at her feet, alert and watching me closely.

It was always the case when a much-loved family pet was surrendered into my care that the owners were visibly upset when I left with the dog. This time was no exception, and the woman showed her emotions, hugging the dog one last time before I put the lead on and started for the door.

As I reached the door, she told me she was leaving for Germany in the morning, and could she ring me before she left to see how the dog had settled in.

Leaving for Germany! Obviously, my next question was, "Did you speak to the dog in German?" and the answer was, "Yes, all the time." The dog's name was Kaiser, which should have given me a clue as to the woman's nationality, but she had no accent, and I had given no thought to where she was travelling.

I then took a closer look at the dog. He was a big and well-built Shepherd, but not of show quality. His left ear drooped at an odd angle; the right ear pricked up when alerted to noise or movement, but the left ear remained down, giving the dog a somewhat comical expression when he was vigilant.

Surprisingly, Kaiser went with me without a problem. On the way to Manfred's place, I stopped and walked Kaiser through a busy shopping centre, over a bridge, and through a pedestrian tunnel to gauge how he reacted to traffic and crowded, noisy situations.

Kaiser was calm but alert, walking beside me and not faltering as we traversed the streets before heading off to Manfred's home.

Manfred, his wife and two very excited young children greeted us at the front door. Kaiser stood calmly beside me, surveying his new family and home and accepting the affection lavished on him by the children.

We entered the lounge room, and I gave them the information I had on the dog's medical, daily care, and feeding regime. Then, I proceeded to give them a run-through of the commands he had been given by his former owners.

Kaiser lay at my feet, initially alert to all that was going on around him, then laid his head next to my feet, obviously relaxed in the new surroundings.

I had explained to Manfred before our arrival that the dog's former owners were German, and the dog was receptive to commands in both German and English. Kaiser's reaction to Manfred changing to German as he spoke to his wife was comical as the dog sprang to his feet and approached Manfred, standing in front of him, cocking his head, then moving over to Manfred's wife as she also replied in German.

Kaiser settled into the household and became a valued member of the family! Manfred left to play in the tournament in Germany, leaving his loved ones protected by Kaiser who proved to be exceptionally protective of the family.

Kaiser finally passed away from old age many years later, a much-loved family pet who had ticked *all* the many boxes of demands made by Manfred in our initial phone conversation.

I am still amazed that what seemed impossible to find *exactly* what Manfred had requested *was* possible!

# MELISSOPHOBIA*

IT WAS A BALMY MORNING, AND I WAS HEADING towards my first appointment of the day. Traffic was light and I manoeuvred my motorcycle through the traffic, enjoying the ride and reflecting on the phone conversation I had with the new client a week earlier.

The client owned an adult male Rottweiler who he stated had become uncontrollable and was showing some aggressive tendencies to both family and visitors.

Rottweilers are one of my favourite breeds, are very receptive to training and usually make a great family pet. They can, however, become very territorial and protective of both their owners and their yard.

From my initial discussion with the owner, I had assumed that as the dog matured and reached its full size that it had challenged the owners, successfully, over a period and become the dominant figure in their pack.

In many cases this situation can be reversed by the dog being obedience-trained, and the owner becoming consistent with commands and learning to handle the dog. Handling and commands are first given with the dog on the lead. When the dog is conditioned to obeying both voice commands and hand signals, the lead is removed, and the owner can then control the dog when it is running free.

To achieve this control, there must be consistency—not only from the handler, but also from family members—or the control breaks down. In this situation, with a big, powerful and supposedly aggressive dog challenging its owners' pack leadership, this scenario could cause major problems.

I had turned into the street by then, and my initial thoughts were that the training should be straightforward. My normal method was to gain control of the dog while it was on a lead, and show it leadership with firm commands and good lead control.

These thoughts were quickly erased from my mind when I pulled up outside of the residence and heard a barrage of very loud and very aggressive barking emanating from behind a wrought iron fence.

I had not yet turned the motor of the bike off when the dog threw itself against the fence, its head above the top rail, its massive body convulsing in a furious display of raw power and fury.

Aggressive dogs were not new to me, as I operated a security company and we trained both dogs for crowd control and detection work, as well as guard dogs which protected factory yards and industrial sites. Many of these dogs were donated to us as they were aggressive and uncontrollable.

I was experienced at handling these dogs and I was usually unfazed—however, in this instance I stood in awe at the speed, power and aggression shown by this magnificent creature.

I watched him for some thirty seconds, expecting the anger to abate if I did not move. No chance. His aggression continued as he frantically jumped at the fence.

A thorough visual showed the fence was strong and would stand the pressure and I also noted there was a very large lock and chain securing the gate.

Fortified with that information I ventured up the pass towards the fence which would allow me to access the veranda and gain entrance through the front door.

Unnoticed by me, the owner had come out and was standing on the veranda, obviously watching the entire proceedings.

It turned out that the man was of Lebanese descent, medium size, and possibly in his early forties.

He introduced himself as George and shook my hand with a firm grip, shaking his head. "That dog is crazy! He was such a beautiful puppy, but now …" His words trailed off and he shrugged his shoulders.

He ushered me inside to a very neat and orderly house and introduced me to his family, wife and two teenage boys. Sitting in the corner was his ninety-five-year-old mother, who smiled and waved to welcome me.

My initial training session usually starts with a consultation where I gather the relevant information regarding the dog's health, any problem areas, and what the owners' expectations are from the training. There was no point in this case; the major problems were obvious.

The dog was big, boisterous, aggressive and incredibly agile—and uncontrollable.

I knew well this was going to be a difficult job. Although I had handled many aggressive dogs before, and was well-versed in all their moves, I never underestimated any new dog that came into my training.

I then asked George to go out into the yard and place a training collar, attached to my six-foot training lead, around the dog's neck and hand me the lead through the door.

By doing this I could step out in the yard and start to work the dog.

George looked at me as if I were insane. "I am not going out there with that Devil dog!" he exclaimed. "He jumps all over me and growls, and I am scared of him!"

It seemed we had reached a stalemate; George would not venture into the yard, and I would not be able to place the collar on the dog without suffering severe bites.

At this point, George's mother volunteered to place the collar on the dog.

I interjected, thinking placing this frail old lady in the position of handling such an aggressive dog was absolute lunacy.

The old lady was determined and shuffled slowly across the floor. She took the lead from George's hand and muttered under her breath.

The dog was patrolling outside the door, growling and obviously agitated, and I was worried about the old lady as she checked with me which way the collar fitted.

The dog's aggression heightened as the door swung open and he was up on his hind legs, ready to lunge.

This appeared to be a one-sided and dangerous confrontation. The dog was like a coiled spring, ready to react to any intrusion on its territory and capable of inflicting serious wounds to any trespasser.

On the other side of the equation, we had a fragile, slow-moving ninety-five-year-old lady as the dog's opposition in what appeared to be a one-sided contest.

Her confidence in handling the situation, and the family seemingly happy for her to approach the dog, eased my mind. I realised that this little, frail old lady was the family matriarch. No longer active in her body, but despite having a beautiful smile and gentle manner, her dominance over the family extended to the dog she had helped raise. She demanded respect and the dog, as a pup, would have been subjected to her discipline— and hopefully react accordingly.

Undaunted, the old lady stepped into the yard and spoke with a firm tone in Lebanese.

Despite the seriousness of the situation the dog's reaction was comical. The dog dropped to the ground immediately in a submissive pose, obviously intimidated by the old lady.

The lead and collar were attached with a little difficulty and the lady stood up and smiled at me through the doorway and handed me the lead. Mission accomplished!

I stepped out into the yard, and as I expected, the dog tried to attack me. As I had stated before, the dog was big, mobile and very aggressive and capable of inflicting serious injuries to an unprotected limb.

I have worked with this type of dog on many occasions over the years. Working them on a lead and keeping them off balance so they cannot bite the handler requires a combination of speed, strength, and agility from the handler—me.

Some breeds of dogs have a very low body sensitivity, and this, coupled with their aggression at the time, makes them very hard to handle. Trainers often use heavy, compulsive methods to subdue the dogs in this situation, which may have side effects on the dog's training or behaviour at a later stage, and in some cases just incite more aggression.

I have found that most dogs cannot sustain this height of aggression for a long period of time, and patience, good handling and some amount of luck from the handler can usually bring the dog under control.

This dog, however, was an exception, and continued to lunge at me and try to bite me. I had been working the dog for three or four minutes and he was not subdued in any way and seemed to have a never-ending stream of raw energy, while in truth *my* store of energy was wilting.

I continually changed directions, evading the attacks and keeping the dog off balance, and gradually gained some control; at this point his aggression eased off and he warily accepted me patting him.

This is often the case, where the dog will accept pack leadership from another dog who is stronger, or a human who can control them.

At this stage, I looked up and noticed something that struck me with abject terror. The dog's owner was a beekeeper, and his flourishing beehive was situated against the fence in his yard, not three metres away from me.

I had been stung by a bee when I was a child and the pain at the time was so severe that the sight of the beehive in such proximity was enough to trigger my fearful reaction. I had maintained that fear of bees ever since. The pain from that sting was recalled instantly to my mind, and over the years I had maintained a dread of being stung again.

It was a moment frozen in time! I—was shocked like a statue, petrified of being stung; the dog sitting beside me, possibly regenerating its energy to attack me again, and the owner watching me with a mystified look.

I stopped dead in my tracks, worried that any quick movement or loud command would provoke an attack by the bees.

The dog's owner had noticed my reaction and asked me what was wrong.

I responded in a very quavering voice, "Will those bees bite me?"

"Mate, the dog is trying to kill you and you are worried about a bee sting? Are you crazy?"

The moment was broken by a warning growl from the dog, who had taken advantage of my lack of concentration and mounted another attack, though not quite as volatile as the first.

That lesson finished with the dog under control on the lead, and he allowed me to handle him in future sessions, only challenging me initially when I placed him in the 'drop' position. He was unhappy at me putting him in a submissive position; it did not sit well with him initially.

This story has a happy ending. The dog responded well to training, retained its protective instincts in the yard, and became a trusted family pet.

The owners became adept handlers, and the family and dog blended into an environment where it accepted the family's control and became a trusted and much-loved family pet. The grandmother remained firmly entrenched as the family matriarch.

*\* This chapter is titled 'Melissophobia', which is the term used for a person afraid of bees.*

# NIGHT SWIM

THIS STORY IS ABOUT ANOTHER TIME when I was operating a security company which hired out guard dogs to industrial sites, building sites and storage yards. Occasionally we received an unusual request; the one in question here nearly cost me my life.

The request for guard dogs came from a company which operated a sand dredging company. The dredge in this case was situated at Kurnell in Sydney's south, where there were, at the time, huge sandhills.

The locals were protesting regarding the sandhills being desecrated. After their vocal protests were ignored on several occasions, the dredge was sabotaged, causing the company to temporarily cease operations while repairs were completed.

I attended the site in daylight hours to survey the area and the needs of the client. I immediately realised this was a difficult job. The dredge was situated in the middle of a man-made lake; the dredge floated in the lake and pumped sand onto the shore where it was loaded and carried away.

To gain access for the dogs I would have to place them in a small tinny boat and row them out to the dredge in the afternoon, and row them back to the on-site kennel early in the morning before the dredging began.

I was confident that the dogs would deter any entry onto the dredge, and they would warn of any attempts by barking and showing aggression to any trespassers on the property.

There were, however, several other problems. Firstly, the safety of the dogs. I would have to train the dogs initially to settle while being rowed out—to get into the small aluminium boat and sit quietly. I did not anticipate a big problem with this, and I had two older dogs in mind who had worked together previously, and I felt would be suitable.

The second problem was that although the dredge was a good size and had a safety fence around the deck, I had to ensure the dogs would not jump into the water and swim back to the shore.

There was adequate shelter to keep the dogs out of the weather, so I was satisfied with that aspect of their safety.

I had a meeting with the foreman of the site and worked out a few details on times, and a placement for a portable kennel, with an exercise yard to be located on site

I kennelled the dogs on site for a few days and rowed them out to the dredge after work had ceased for the day without incident.

The dogs were on site for a few weeks and there were no further incidents from the saboteurs. The dogs were happy to sleep the time away through the day, only waking to warn off any workmen who ventured too close to their kennel.

A few weeks into the job, I received a request from the site asking to place the dogs on the dredge at a later time. The foreman explained that there was some ongoing maintenance being completed that would not be finished for the normal time, and apologised for any inconvenience.

I agreed to this request and travelled to the site at the appointed time, arriving in darkness. I was not overly concerned regarding the change of routine; however, I was certainly concerned about the weather.

It was August, which is traditionally the month where we get the most wind, and the dredge was dwarfed in between two monstrous sandhills that towered over it.

The wind had picked up speed and whistled down through the sandhills which formed a natural corridor, churning the top of the water into small, white-capped waves.

I surveyed the scene, deciding on the best course of action to take, realising that the dredge was anchored much nearer to the tallest sandhill than it had been previously.

The risk factor had increased slightly but I could see no danger to the dogs, so I loaded them onto the small boat and started the short row to the dredge.

We approached the dredge, and I lifted them on and then checked the deck for their shelter and left water for them. As I was pushing the boat away, a wall of the sandhill closest to the boat collapsed and an enormous amount of sand crashed down into the water, causing a mini tidal wave that crashed into the side of the boat.

There was no impending warning of the avalanche, I was taken completely by surprise— still standing, as I had just pushed off from the dredge. The wave smashed into the side of the little tinny with such force I overbalanced and fell, hitting my head on the side of the boat and then toppling over the side into the ice-cold winter water.

I was initially stunned by the blow to the head but quickly reacted to the freezing-cold water. I had heavy, warm clothing on and realised I would not have the strength to last long in the cold water as my clothing was weighing me down.

The boat was just out of my reach, and as I struggled towards it, I was already losing strength and the temperature of the water was really affecting my coordination.

Another wave hit the boat and propelled it towards me, and I managed to grab hold of the side as *another* avalanche hit the water, and the wave pushed both the boat and me closer to the shore.

I looked back towards the dredge and the dogs were steady on their feet and seemed unaware of any danger.

Looking over my shoulder I could see we had drifted closer to the shore and with a few more strokes I was able to drag myself onto the sand.

I lay there, the combination of the fatigue and the cold almost paralysing me, and it was some time before I had the energy to walk back to the car.

I had the keys to the work shed which had showers and I managed to get over to the shed with the intention of having a hot shower to regain my strength as the cold was causing me to shiver uncontrollably by that time.

Placing the key in the lock was a major problem as my hands were shaking and I had no control over my fingers; I fumbled with the keys and lock for what seemed an eternity. Finally, I gained entry, and had a long, hot shower before finding some dry clothes left by the workmen.

Still fatigued and shaken I returned to the car and realised I was in no fit state to drive. I used the two-way radio to contact our night patrolman and organised him to get a casual in to cover the rest of my shift

I managed to secure the tinny to the dock before returning to the work shed and spending the night in front of a heater, waiting for the morning shift to arrive

I had recovered sufficiently to row out and retrieve the dogs before the workers arrived, and I informed them of what had happened and the fact I had used a worker's clothes.

They sympathised with me as I told them my story, and we organised that the dredge would not be left so close to the wall in the future.

I finally drove home that day realising just how *lucky* I had been—*miles* from any other person, with no chance of *any* aid. I had been very fortunate to survive.

Years later I was driving down the road and the huge sandhills had disappeared. Much of it had been used for manufacturing glass and more was exported to top up other beaches. I was stunned at the difference; those big, beautiful, majestic sandhills were no more, and I was saddened that I had been part of their destruction, as they had almost been part of *my own* destruction those many years ago.

# NIGHT TEST

THE TRAINING OF DOGS FOR SECURITY PATROL WORK involves many facets of training that are not at all obvious to people unfamiliar with this type of training. Before the dog is regarded as having achieved a suitable standard, it must show the ability, willingness and courage to perform the search patrol, attack and arrest sequences.

Many dogs who work well in daylight do not perform as well at night when their senses are more acute. The handler's ability to adapt at night is also important, because if the handler is nervous, the dog will pick up on this, and may not react well.

My first ever fully trained patrolled dog was a German Shepherd named Bull. Bull was a short, stocky dog and had the ideal temperament for patrol work. We had undergone an intensive training course at Mal's Animals Agency complex, and after weeks of obedience training and attack work, we were ready for our passing-out test.

Mal is an ex-Royal Airforce dog trainer instructor, and is a stickler for detail—and he demanded the same standards for any handler he instructs.

The day of the test, I was somewhat nervous. The obedience, agility and attack test were all completed successfully, leaving only the night test left.

There were several hours of daylight left and I was examined on my knowledge of wind scenting and arrest procedures by way of written examination before night closed in, allowing for the night test to begin. Mal had given the explicit instructions regarding the test; I had memorised all the details and was looking forward to completing the test, and working on patrol work the following evening.

I had developed a strong relationship with Bull, and I never gave any thought to the fact that he may not stand up to the pressure of a night test.

The area where the test was to be conducted was a five-acre paddock. A drum had been placed in the middle of the area, with an object on top. The idea was that the two criminals would try and breach the area and steal the object, before being detected by the team of Bull and me.

The patrolling of an area is a team effort, so Bull and I would have to patrol effectively if we wanted to keep intruders away from the drum. We were not allowed to stay in close proximity to the drum but patrol the whole area, and endeavour to catch the criminals close to the boundary.

Instructions completed, Bull and I ventured forth, brimming with confidence at our ability as a good team to secure the area.

It was a pitch-black night, ideal for this type of test. We moved into the test area and I walked through strips of dense fog that hung heavily in small pockets, seeping through my coat and chilling my bones.

Visibility was poor, and I realised that I was very dependent upon Bull's keen sense of smell and acute hearing. I had surveyed the area in daylight, and I worked out my method of patrol. I tested the wind and started on my first patrol pattern, winding my way across the paddock, intent on detecting every sound, searching for any movement within or near the area.

The minutes ticked by, and my first feelings of expectancy and anticipation were dulled as a wet chill seeped through my clothes. My feet had also become wet, and I was becoming increasingly cold and uncomfortable. Still, I had a job to do, and I was *determined* that Bull and I would pass out with very high marks, so I plodded on, trying to blot out the physical discomfort and concentrate on the job at hand.

Bull showed no reaction to the cold, and was obviously happy with my company, and he maintained an alert air, occasionally sniffing in one direction or another. Bull's attitude encouraged me, and I had no doubt that he would acquit himself well in the expected attack sequence.

The test and the training were made as realistic as possible, and the chances of confronting a criminal trying to break into a factory while on patrol work were high, hence the test being carried out in this way.

I had lost track of time, but I estimated that I had been in the area for over an hour. My ego told me that the criminals had not been able to gain access to the area because of the effective patrol method I was using to secure the area.

In fact, the criminals were sitting up in a house by the open fire, drinking copious quantities of tea while watching a movie. When the movie was over, they reluctantly ventured out into the cold night air.

After patrolling for all this time, I started to become a little disorientated, as well as cold and miserable, and I longed to be home with a cup of tea and the night papers.

Then I heard a noise and my nerves sharpened, and I watched Bull to see if he indicated that he had picked up the scent.

He did not, and I relaxed and continued. I neared a clump of trees which I thought would be the obvious place for the criminals to hide, and stopped momentarily to listen for any sound that would determine the presence of intruders.

At that moment a figure ran out from the bushes; the face was illuminated and distorted, maniacal eyes reflected the torch and there was wailing like a banshee—the sight and sound was awesome!

I didn't realise at that moment that it was Mal, and he had held the torch upwards under his chin, so that it shone up into his face.

This is not at all what I expected; I had expected search and arrest procedure without this, and the shock was too much for my system. I didn't hesitate, I dropped Bull's lead and ran blindly up the paddock, tripping over and skinning my knees before scrambling forward, endeavouring to put as much distance between me and whatever it was back there.

Bull, to his eternal credit, stood his ground and moved forward towards the figure. This had all taken place in only a few seconds, and at this point, I heard Mal's laughter booming across the paddock—and I realised what had happened.

I returned sheepishly to my dog and picked up the lead from the other 'criminal' who had handled Bull prior to my training. Mal was doubled up laughing at my expense, and I stood there—hurt that the test was not carried out as it had been explained. I was also embarrassed, of course, and I must be the only handler in history to fail a night test when his dog passed with flying colours!

I still have Bull's test sheet, almost fifteen years later; we scored a commendable 87 out of 100. The 13 points were lost due to my performance in the night test.

Bull has passed on to his final resting place, but that dog gave me many years of faithful service, and never once let me down.

And thinking back on our night test, I wish I could say the same thing to you, old mate!

# THE DOGGA NO STAY

MANY PEOPLE ARE FIRMLY CONVINCED THAT the saying 'You can't teach an old dog new tricks' is quite correct. Well, I don't believe that this is quite true. Older dogs are more set in their ways, sure, and not as impressionable as youngsters, but I have trained many older dogs who have reached creditable standards.

One such dog springs to mind. A young Italian youth rang me regarding his six-year-old male German Shepherd. The dog had been confined to a yard for all of his life, and had become a problem because of his consistent barking. The dog had not been a problem until the family moved house, and the dog felt insecure in his new yard and so barked continuously.

Walking the dog on the lead was not possible, as the dog had never been on a lead and the owner had no control when he had tried.

I suggested that I take the dog to the kennels on a weekly basis to see if he was receptive to, and capable of, retaining training. The dog proved to be *more* than capable, and by the end of the normal six-week training period, he was predictable with on-lead work, and was confident around traffic, and every other daytime street distraction.

The youth rang me on the night he picked the dog up, delighted that the dog was able to be walked down to the local park and exercised on an extended lead. The boy had shown an ability to handle his dog on a demonstration, and I was pleased with the overall effort.

My pleasure was short-lived when the next morning, very early, I had a phone call from his irate mother who screamed down the phone, "You a badda man, you takka my boy's money, and you donta do a job on the dogga, just lika you say. Thissa dogga not a trainna like you say, no way, he notta do whatta I tell himma to do, no way ..."

This was long before the days of a Consumer Affairs Department, but the threat of exposure to all and sundry was loud and clear.

"I'm a gonna ringa the papers, I'm a gonna ringa Mr John Laws, I'm a gonna tell him, he fixa you good, I am a gonna tell you that's a for sure."

At this stage, I tried to interject, but the lady was too excited to listen. I tried again moments later. "The dog was demonstrated to your son when you weren't here, you did not have a session to be taught how to handle the dog, and if you wish to come up on the weekend, I will demonstrate the dog working and instruct you on how to handle it," I said with as much patience as I could muster.

At this point, I could not believe the lady was *not* happy with the result. The dog was not predictable in its off-lead heel work, as its concentration had not been developed due to age and narrow development, but the overall result, even to someone inexperienced, was *obvious*.

Her reply to my offer boomed down the phone: "No way I'm a gonna come all the way up there, Mister, I wasta enough money, you a understand me?"

I decided to try a new course of questioning, and established *exactly* what the dog would not do. "The dogga no do what he a told," I was told loudly.

"Exactly *what* won't it do?" I asked with frustration.

"The dogga no stay," the lady said.

This may have been because the lady wasn't handling the dog correctly, or because she expected the dog to work perfectly around distraction.

This is one of the problems faced by people with older dogs—training the dogs to hold concentration is difficult, and the one thing a trainer can't do is give the dog extended experience. I had already explained that to her son. "Okay," I said thoughtfully. "But exactly *what* did you do when the dog wouldn't stay?"

The women was obviously frustrated with my stupidity; she took a deep breath before replying. "Donna you maka excuses to me mister, lasta night before I go to bed, see the dogga in the kennel lying down, I tell him to 'stay there', this morning I getta up, and he runna all over the backa yard, he not trained mister!"

# WATERPROOF

ONE EVENING I RECEIVED A TELEPHONE CALL from a friend enquiring whether I could assist him in finding a home for a seven-year-old German Shepherd bitch. The dog's owner had been forced to move and couldn't accommodate the dog in his new home. The family were very attached to the dog and had so far been unsuccessful in finding a new home.

I jotted down some information about the dog's background as we talked and then arranged to pick her up early the next morning. As we drove that morning, I ran into a fierce storm, black clouds hovering ominously while the wind lashed the rain against the windscreen, dramatically reducing visibility.

The address I had been given was a beachside suburb with the street located right at the beachfront. I located it without much trouble and pulled up in the street beside the house facing the ocean. The seas were heavy and raging, the beach devoid of any human form, in complete contrast to a sunny day when people crammed every available position. The heavy rolling cloud banks and pelting rain only added to the spectacle and made me aware of the incredible might of the sea and the elements.

As I sat taking in the view, I noticed a utility outside the house filled with an amazing assortment of garden equipment and household effects. A lady and two men were working in the yard stacking furniture under the cover of the carport.

The rain stopped as I alighted from the car and walked towards the house; the lady saw me approaching and turned to meet me at the gate. She introduced herself as the daughter of the man surrendering the dog. She was visibly upset, her eyes moist and her voice trembling slightly as she fought to control her emotions before a stranger.

I had encountered this sadness often when I picked up a dog which had to be surrendered. I have seen grown men break down and cry on numerous occasions, and women and children sob hysterically. Some react differently and withdraw in silence, while others seem glad that the dog is going. It is something I have never grown accustomed to—the emotional strain when a dog is parted from its family.

I have developed a system in these pick-ups where I get as much information as I can *before* I arrive, and get in and out quickly, without getting involved in any way. I had made the mistake early when I stood around and talked, trying to placate anxious owners—only making the situation worse for everyone concerned. I now take the view that I should *not* get involved, no matter *what!*

The lady ushered me through the garage which was under the main structure of the house. The house itself was a huge rambling weatherboard of post-World War II design, sitting in the middle of a large block of land, and had a nice secure family atmosphere about it. The owners were obviously 'collectors' and over a period of many years had accumulated an incredible array of bits and pieces, which were stacked neatly around the garage area and the yard.

The lady then turned and faced me, wringing her hands and apologising for being so upset. What she told me explained her sadness over and above the surrender of the dog. Her seventy-nine-year-old father had built the house forty-one years ago and raised his family there. The house was the first in the street and a landmark in the area, with spectacular views of the coastline from almost every room.

The government had resumed the land to extend the parkland, and the old man had fought and lost a bitter ten-year battle to retain his home. The compensation did not take into consideration the lost value of position and would not even buy a decent home in the area where he had spent so many years. The old man was moving to a home unit in a distant suburb.

I reacted inwardly to the coldness of a bureaucratic machine that could take away a family home with the stroke of a pen—not for an essential hospital site, but for a parkland of which there was an abundance along the beachfront. What consideration is given to human suffering when these decisions are made, I wondered? Did some public servant living in a lesser location make the decision out of envy? Was there a real need to uproot an old man in his golden years in the cause of environmental progress?

I pondered these questions as the lady told me her story. They had fought until the last, but had been issued with a court order to vacate by noon that day.

The dog was called in and stood aloof, eyeing me cautiously before moving forward and sniffing my outstretched hand. She gained confidence and nuzzled my hand for attention as I knelt down beside her. The lady was obviously pleased with the dog's response, who placed her paw on my shoulder and tried to lick my face.

The dog walked readily on the lead beside me as we made our way through the stacked-up furniture and other objects which were piled up ready for loading.

As we walked up the drive, the old man stood watching us, hands on his hips, his large frame stooped with age but still showing the virile strength of years gone by.

He straightened up and walked slowly down the drive and stood before me, patting the dog gently. He had not said a word to me, but I knew him for the man he was by his stance and action. Thick grey hair receding slightly crowned a weather-beaten, open face with a large broad nose and blue eyes that met mine directly.

This was a man from my dad's era. Men who had fought for Australia in two world wars and had raised their families during the Depression and post war years. They had worked their forty-eight-hour week and had none of the benefits of shift allowances, leave loadings or four weeks' annual leave, but worked good, honest lives, battling to raise and provide for a family in difficult times.

He held out a large, calloused hand, gripping me with a strength that was not at all surprising. "Thanks, mate, you're all right. I can see that she will go to a good home!"

Having said that, he patted his dog once more and walked away so he wouldn't betray his feelings.

I loaded the dog in the car and the lady ran down with a can of food and some dog biscuits.

"Thanks for your trouble," she said, choking back the tears and placing her hands over her face.

"No trouble," I said. "Good luck." I drove up the road as the old man began loading his truck.

Inside I was seething at the old man's misfortune. losing both his home and his dog. The rain started again as I relived the look of anguish in the eyes of a proud old-timer who had been dispossessed but still retained his strength of character that is typical of his era. I knew instinctively he had seen much hardship over his life and he had handled it the same way as he would handle this set of circumstances.

The wind smashed the rain down as I turned into the shopping centre and headed for home, dog by my side, chastising myself for breaking my own rule of not getting involved.

🐾🐾

# MONTE

ONE DAY, I WAS SITTING IN MY OFFICE catching up on some paperwork when I received a call regarding a seven-year-old aggressive male Great Dane. The caller said he thought the dog would make a good guard dog, and we might be interested in him for our guard dog service.

Great Danes are a beautiful breed and not usually aggressive, so it was an unusual request. I hesitated for a moment and collected my thoughts. There were several problems with agreeing to accept the dog into our care.

The dog was past middle age and would be expensive not only to feed, but possibly also for expensive veterinary treatment. Just the size of the dog would cause us more problems, and the short coat made it susceptible to pressure sores from hard ground and skin allergies from some of the areas they guard.

I thanked the caller for the enquiry but declined the offer; he immediately replied, "That's a shame, I will have to shoot him."

I hesitated a moment before replying, "No, I will take him."

The dog was situated in Lismore, on the north coast of NSW, an eight-hour drive from Sydney where I lived. We arranged to have the dog transported on the train in the luggage compartment, and I was to pick him up from Strathfield station in suburban Sydney when the train arrived the next day at 7:00 a.m.

As I gave the situation more thought, the problems compounded. I had to drive in peak-hour traffic, find parking near a very busy railway station, then pick up a large and aggressive dog and walk it through a crowded area.

Still, the dog would be getting a reprieve from being put down, and if worse came to worst, he could live out his life in the kennels and exercise yards at my training compound.

I arrived at the station the next morning, parked the car, and gathered my lead and a leather slip collar and walked up onto the station platform.

The platform was crowded with commuters and school children milling around, and I picked my way through people, young and old, and the many school bags that littered the area.

The train was supposed to arrive and the dog unloaded by 7:15 a.m.; however, by 8:00 a.m., although five trains had arrived and departed, there was still no sign of the dog.

As I stood waiting and wondering how they were going to unload the dog onto the platform, I heard a young girl scream loudly from the platform opposite. Some other schoolgirls were giggling and backing away from a caged area on the platform where luggage and parcels were stored—along with a huge, muzzled Great Dane standing on its back legs, its front paws on the wire.

There was no doubt this was Monte, muzzled with a sturdy, home-made muzzle and looking very stressed. I reacted quickly, made my way to the platform, and spoke to the attendant working in the caged area.

By this time, Monte had lain down and was panting heavily, looking very weak. The long train trip in a hot, confined carriage had obviously affected him.

I gave him a quick inspection and took the chance of removing the muzzle and giving him water. Monte drank a copious amount of water which I fed to him in small amounts while patting him and talking to him.

Monte was a fine specimen with a huge head and chest. I sat beside him while he recovered. I asked the attendant how Monte had arrived on this side of the line. He informed me because there was no cage on the opposite side the dog had been taken to Central

Station in the city, and dropped off on the return leg to this side.

By this stage Monte had recovered and was standing up; up to this point he had shown no aggression, until I went to put the muzzle on him.

Monte let me know—both with his body language and a low, meaningful growl—that he was not going to be muzzled again.

The platform was still crowded. I dared not walk a supposedly aggressive dog through a crowded station area without a muzzle.

I explained my predicament to the attendant who waited till the next train left and ushered me down the platform, now nearly devoid of passengers, and through a side gate that led me to the road near where my truck was parked.

Monte walked alongside me on a slack lead, not pulling and seemingly content now he was unmuzzled and away from the train station. I approached the truck and went to place him in the rear compartment.

Bad mistake on my part—Monte's aggression flared again as he reared up, snarling and growling. I walked him away from the truck and controlled him quickly, and he quieted down. I patted him and soothed him vocally.

It was obvious that he would not go into a confined space again, and I was now in a quandary about how to transport him. I was 30 km away from my kennels, and I could not leave him while I went to get an open-caged trailer, which I had at the property.

I walked him to the front of the truck, and he sat near the front door wagging his tail, so I opened the door and he tried to jump onto the front seat. With my help with his back legs, he adjusted his huge body and sat looking out the windscreen!

I had a previous experience with another dog I owned—Bear had also refused to enter the kennels on the back of the truck and always sat beside me, with his head on my lap.

Monte was obviously no stranger to the front seat of a truck, and made himself comfortable lying across the seat as Bear had done, with his head on my lap.

The trip home was uneventful, and Monte settled in with me, adjusting well to life in the kennels and accompanying me every afternoon when I left the property to work my security shift.

Monte proved to be a faithful companion, following me around the kennels through the day and showing many of Bear's traits which endeared him to me even more.

In the afternoons, when I was preparing to leave to release dogs on the sites, Monte would sit or lie down patiently beside the truck until it was time to leave.

Monte would sleep contentedly in the truck, only raising his head occasionally to make himself more comfortable. While he was protective on the property, Monte *never* showed the aggression that he reputedly had before he came into my care.

Except on occasions when I teased him occasionally by opening the back kennel of the truck and telling him to get in, he would then walk to the front of the truck and sit, waiting to be lifted into his seat.

Monte was approximately seven when I obtained him and, therefore, around ten when he passed away overnight of old age; he had slowed down over the last few months but showed no sign of pain and was still eating well.

I had taken him down to the kennels on a rare night we had off, and he came over as I was leaving

and nuzzled into my leg, looking for his last pat at night, as usual. I patted him and left, not knowing this would be the last time I had that opportunity.

I have owned many dogs in my life, and the best ones have always come to me in odd circumstances. Monte was undoubtedly one of the *best,* and I was fortunate he came into my life, and we were able to spend so much quality time together.

For those of you who have been blessed to have a special dog in your life, you will understand my sense of great privilege in having Monte's company, even if only for three years.

# About the Author

Jim Fraser was a professional dog trainer for more than two decades, after resigning from the NSW Police Force to establish a private security company utilising dogs.

This evolved into an interest in kennels and dealing with behavioural problems for domestic pets through home training programs at which he had a close-up look at dogs in a family situation. He operated a canine behaviour clinic for the NSW RSPCA and was a consultant to the Guide Dogs for the Blind. He co-authored *My Dog*, a canine behaviour guide with veterinarian the late Dr Pam Tinslay. Jim's work with dogs was stopped suddenly after a motor cycle accident.

Jim also runs a successful goalkeeping clinic and oversees the Women's National Premier League, Academy, and Goalkeeper development programs for Western Sydney Wanderers A-League club. He has previously worked with the Australian and Philippine national football teams. He played football in the NSW state league and played ten games for the Socceroos from 1973-74.

# More really good books from Fair Play Publishing

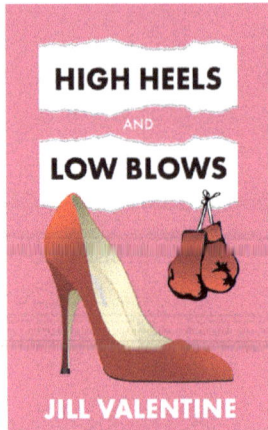

**High Heels and Low Blows**
By Jill Valentine

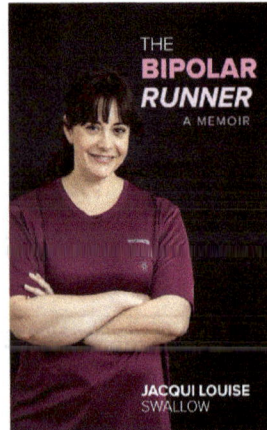

**The Bipolar Runner**
By Jacqui Louise Swallow

**Turning the Tide**
By Michelle Ford-Eriksson

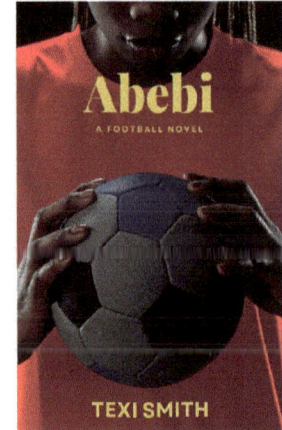

**Abebi**
By Texi Smith

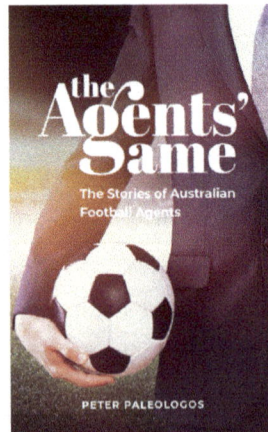

**The Agents' Game**
By Peter Paleologos

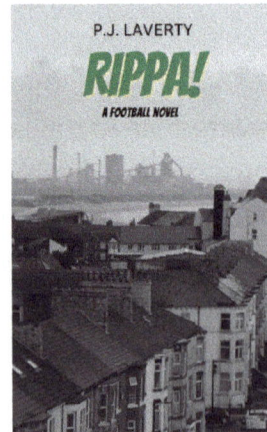

**RIPPA!**
By P.J. Laverty

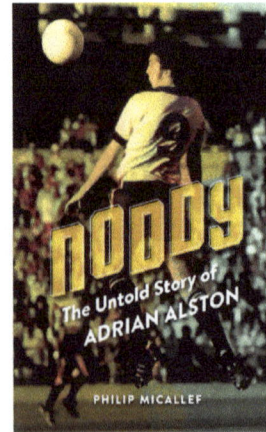

**Noddy**
By Philip Micallef

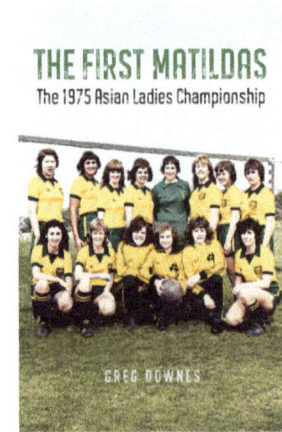

**The First Matildas**
By Greg Downes

Available from
fairplaypublishing.com.au
and all good bookstores

FAIRPLAY
PUBLISHING

9 781925 914993